SHADOW BOUND

SHADOW BOUND CHRONICLES
BOOK 1

A. L. SCARBOROUGH

For Bubba & Zeke

DON'T MISS MY NEW RELEASES

Join the A.L. Scarborough Chronicles email list to get exclusive access to updates on my latest works in progress, new characters, character profile art, behind-the-scenes peeks, and new releases.

https://www.aliciascarborough.com/sign-up.html

CONTENTS

CHAPTER
ONE

He was late. My time in this small town was at the end and he was late. Walter, my bastard of a husband, was toying with my fixation of a sure bet. He said it was a done deal and I would be free to leave the supernatural underworld mafia with no strings attached. Fat lot that was and I was a fool to have believed him.

On my wrists were tattooed two dice that symbolized my vice. Everyone had something different. Walter's was a stack of cash. Snaking up my right arm was a snake tattoo that wrapped around it several times. It was a magical tattoo that grew when you crossed the mafia. Once the snake's head kissed your neck it would inject the deadly venom that would stop your heart. That's how the mafia took out their turncoats.

Mine was almost at my neck. Walter said that he knew someone who could remove them. That was why we were holed up in this dump. That and the solid cement floor. It was less likely for supernatural spies to burst through a solid floor that was one hundred percent cement.

The air conditioner unit rattled like a half-dead drummer that missed a few beats between each measure and carried on with no worries. The constant chonk de chonk chonk da langa langa lang lang thrummed throughout the room. Though the temperature kept at a balmy eighty degrees despite the AC unit's best attempts.

Humidity was palatable making one consider reaching for scuba gear to survive the onslaught of water winning over the ratio of breathable air. If you could even call the air breathable.

Musty smells from over exuberant humans in the throws of primal pleasure soaked the yellow watered stained outdated wallpaper. The bedsheets fared no better. Though the smell of collected stale pizza crusts within old boxes stacked over in the far corner of the room added to the ambiance.

I held fast in the old wicker chair that was once painted black and breathed through my mouth. The paint chipped where past human contact wore it raw with acidic oils. I shifted in the seat which creaked with the new strain of weight on the old wicker reeds. I probably needed to go on a diet. Maybe.

Overhead the exposed pipes once hidden by long gone ceiling tiles were wet with condensation as the room's temperature fought to be comfortable. Water dripped down onto the table, close to the cards laid out in a spread of solitaire. I steepled my fingers, leaned forward and surveyed the hand dealt.

Under the table, my foot tapped and tried to keep time with the erratic AC unit. I ticked my eyes over to the door that led outside. Another wicker chair was wedged up under the handle. Not that it would keep anyone out, but it would delay them just enough for me to make my escape out the bathroom window.

I reached out to turn the next card in the pile when the door slammed open. My heart lunged into my throat, and I leapt away from the entrance. The wicker chair that was wedged under the door splintered into thousands of pieces. It never had a chance—the same for my escape.

A heavy weight pummeled into my midsection and careened us both backwards into the bed. The comforter cushioned the blow to the back of my head when we came to stop against the wall. Cracks within the wall and broken sheetrock marked the landing site of my skull.

The weight groaned and rolled over. Though I helped and pushed him completely off of me. Blood marred the front of my white shirt in a long trail from the impact and upwards to my chest. Are you kidding me? This was a limited edition Gucci shirt and now it was ruined.

Blurred vision played at the edges of my sight, but I shook my head to clear it. Ugh. Should not have done that for now the room spun.

Two hulking goons blocked the door and glowered at me. I swiped at my eyes once more to try and clear my vision. The light tap of high stilettos clicked against the cement walkway outside that led up to the room's entrance. Even with the high pitch rattles and coughs of the overworked AC I knew her footsteps anywhere.

Avarice.

If she was here, then that meant Walter failed and my so-called freedom was a pipe dream.

The dark lump to my side groaned. I chanced a peek at him. Lacerations across his eyebrows, the bridge, an obviously broken nose continued to trickle blood down his unshaven face. Both eyes were swollen shut. The once perfect smile was replaced by the shattered remains of his teeth.

For land's sake Walter, could you do nothing right? I meant you had one job and you screwed that up… royally. Now look at you. Ugh. You better hope that you don't get barfed on by me.

Outside her steps paused, I did not want to look up because I knew that she was at the doorway and waiting for my response. I had crossed her, and this was only the start of her prescript punishment.

"I knew if I followed the rat that I'd eventually find the other one," she drawled.

My fingers curled up in the sweat soaked dirt ridden sheets. A scowl wormed its way onto my face. This was the start of Avarice's torment for those who betrayed her. The taste of lost freedom was bitter ash.

"Darling," Avarice purred. "Look at me."

It wasn't a request but more of a command. Her voice compelled those around her to do as she requested. Resistance was fraught with unease. Your prime directive was to please her and to make her happy.

I propped myself up on one elbow and laid my other hand on top of Walter. His ragged breaths wheezed through bloodied lips. My head leaned to one side and brought the Kingpin of Greed into view. Her mouth split into a wide stunning smile.

She wore all white. The expensive custom-tailored suit hugged her narrow curves down to the expensive six-inch heels that adorned her feet. Avarice was older and had her long silver hair pinned back into a tight bun. Though with her, age did not matter, she didn't need makeup to appear younger to gain favor with the men around her. For she ruled with an iron fist and those loyal were rewarded.

And those that weren't?

Let's just say that the acrid scent of her shambling slaves outside the room gave away the details of my soon-to-be nightmarish future. Their muffled grunts and cries for brains didn't give much room for hope. I shuddered.

Her laugh echoed off the peeling wallpapered walls and fell in time with the off-beat AC unit. There was something off about Avarice that I was never able to pinpoint. No, it wasn't the fact that she had an army of undead minions at her disposal. It was something else.

"What's the matter, Sarah?" Avarice said. "You look a little green around the gills, dear."

My eyes kept watch on the doorway and I held my breath. Not like it mattered. Eventually, I would have to suck in more of the pungent sweet stench of rotted flesh and allow the burn to spread through my parched throat.

Walter moaned again and tried to get up. I pushed him back down on the bed. He always had terrible timing and a fat lot if I was going to suffer his whining along with Avarice's champion crowing. Yes, she had won. She knew she had won.

Desiccated fingers, well, three of them and a stump, wrapped around the door jamb. The creature groaned, jerked forward and lurched to a stop before his master. I knew who this thing used to be and time did no favors for this poor schmuck who was the last to cross Avarice.

He held out a small silver compact phone to her and waited with his head bowed.

"Ah, thank you, Markus." She turned and plucked the device from his grasp. One finger still wrapped around, gave an audible pop and followed the phone.

She wrinkled her nose then shook the phone to knock the appendage off. The finger sailed towards the ground and plopped unceremoniously into the dirt. Her slave didn't mind.

With a flick she opened the phone, pressed one number and brought it to her ear. Her eyes still trained on me and Walter in the motel bed. The AC unit rattled faster in time as though it was listening in on my heart rate. If we moved to attempt an escape she would sic her undead minions on us.

Hmm, what if I threw Walter at them? Would I make it to the bathroom? Did I have enough time to squeeze through the small window of the bathroom before her goons busted down the door? Maybe. Though the odds were not in my favor.

Avarice held up one finger out to us. The universal sign of one moment please. Sure, not like I had anywhere else to go. Just figuring out how to hedge my bets when it came to saving my own skin. Would Walter mind being my shield against the undead?

The tapping of expensive stilettos brought me back. Who in the world was she talking to? Not many people could offset her mood. Avarice's eyes darted from us to her two goons and motioned for them to leave.

More undead shuffled into the goons' vacated space. Some of them I recognized but many were too far gone to identify. The one closest to the door swiveled his head towards the room and leered at me. Eep.

She snapped the phone closed and pocketed it. Her hands smoothed over the unwrinkled suit before she looked up. The smile had worn off and the stern resting bitch face was plastered in its place.

Walter groaned and mumbled, "Invite her in."

"She's not a vampire, Walter," I said.

He winced in pain and hissed between his missing teeth. "Don't matter. Invite her in."

More tapping. Oh for the love of—

"You'd best do as he says Sarah," Avarice said as she waited for me to invite her into the safety of my crummy motel room. It was a rat's nest but it was my rat's nest. Though there was no threshold and she could, if she wanted to, walk in.

I grumbled and pushed myself up to a seated position on the bed. Much better in this position to bolt if needed. I still kept a firm grip on Walter's black tailored coat. My long dirty blonde hair swished in front of my face and I raked it back.

"I'm waiting."

If I got this wrong then I was good as dead. With a roll of my eyes I exhaled and said aloud, "Oh, gracious Kingpin of Greed, Avarice, I entreat you to enter my domain and discuss current matters in a civilized manner. Should I, your host, be ungracious to thee during the time here within these grounds then I forfeit what is mine for you to use as you please."

Walter hissed in a low whisper, "Laying it on a bit thick, ain't ye?"

I elbowed him.

He exhaled with a whine of pain.

"Ah, thank you, my lovely." Avarice's dark rose red lips quirked up at one side as she slightly bowed her head towards me. Heavy footsteps plodded quickly to the opened door. The goons that left earlier appeared in the opening. Avarice pointed her finger towards the bed and said, "Take her."

Her two goons rushed in, oh crap, and snatched me by the arms before I even had time to say 'Jack Rabbit.' Their large rough hands gripped around my biceps and squeezed to ensure I would not slither out of their grasps. I winced and said, "Ouch, easy big guys. There's plenty of me to go around."

The one on my left shot me a nasty glare, squeezed harder to enforce his lack of humor, and then snapped his attention back to his boss. Behind me, on the bed, Walter's ragged breathing kept in time with the lousy AC unit. There was no point in hoping that he'd pull a miraculous rescue on my behalf. Too bad I didn't just leave earlier when things felt like they had gone south.

Her long stilettos clacked against the well worn faded vinyl flooring that was in need of some serious cleaning. The last few years of crud had created a sticky veneer that pulled at her shoes and gave that added clack-stick sound. Cockroaches scurried to their hiding places upon feeling the footsteps. Avarice came to a stop right in front of me.

Green eyes the colors of new dollar bills glared deep into the depths of my soul. Nothing, of course, happened unless you counted the sting of the sudden slap across my face. She held her hand aloft, waited for me to bring my face back around and backhanded me with the same hand.

"Ouch," I said then giggled. Hey, don't blame me. When things get tense my dark sense of humor has a tendency to crop up. "Well, this is awkward, but boss, I don't know how to tell you this… I'm not into S&M."

Another spring of pain bloomed fresh on my cheek once more. Coppery tang mingled with saliva from my split lip. I spat blood onto the floor aiming for her expensive heels. Missed. Avarice's mouth pursed into a scowl while her eyes dared me to speak once more.

After a moment, she lowered her hand because yours truly kept her mouth shut.

"I'm disappointed in you dear," she said, "Did you really think you could get away with it?"

"Not sure what you're talking about. And by the way, I don't consider this to be civilized," I complained.

Her well manicured soft but firm hand took hold of my chin and jerked it to face her. The scowl deepened threatening to make the creases around her mouth and eyes permanent residents.

"Listen to me, Sarah," she started. "You were the one who screwed up. You knew that when you saw me. Those supposed civilized agreements were null and void when you betrayed me."

"I still don't know what you're talking about," I lied.

She released my chin, patted my left cheek, and chuckled. "You do. That's why your heart is racing my dear. And why the snake is almost at your neck. My partners confirmed your recent shady dealings that you were doing behind my back."

My heart lurched to a stop and did a somersault before it labored onward. Cripes.

Should I fess up? No. It was Walter's idea to mess with her records. Not mine. I would't go down because he screwed up. I knew that she had a security system in place. He was foolish to think he could hire some person on XtraHands to do the hacking for him.

"Now tell me, Sarah." Avarice narrowed her eyes. "Why should I let you continue breathing?"

With a witty reply I said, "Um."

"Augh, Morningstar." She spat. "Is that all?"

Okay, time for plan B. I worried my bottom lip, looked over my shoulder at Walter who continued his struggling breath between bloody gasps for air and back to Avarice.

I licked my lips and said, "Um, I'll sell you Walter. That's what you want, right? I sell you him and um, er, I can leave."

"Now, just hold on a wee minute lass—" Walter tried to say and shot up. He appeared to make a sudden recovery.

Avarice interrupted. "You've already sold me Walter."

Walter's head snapped to me and he sputtered. Blood and saliva flew. "What?"

He sagged right back down onto the bed and passed out. I ducked my head. Sorry, Walter.

"Err. Um." My brain told my mouth to reply. Brilliant words really, used to stall the conversation while the rest of my noggin tried to figure out plan C.

"Enough," she barked, turned around, and motioned with her hands. "Bring them."

The goons moved forward, and my battered tennis shoes

squeaked and slid over the vinyl flooring. Even though it was sticky it did not stop these guys from dragging me from the room. Several zombies shambled in after us into the room to grab Walter.

Cool humid air announced the goons' success in pulling me outside. The cicadas rattled loud in the evening as the moon rose into the night sky.

"Whoa, whoa, whoa. Wait," I shouted and kicked my feet in front of me to slow their progress. "Can't we make a deal, boss?"

She was a few steps ahead of us and waggled her index finger in the air. "Too late."

"No, nothing is ever late… remember, boss? You told me that."

"There's a first time for everything."

The goons bundled me out the door and held me higher. They didn't want to chance my glorious feet from tripping them on the way out to the vehicle. Her white limo idled in the parking lot and the doors opened on their own accord.

Behind me I heard several series of thuds as the zombies dragged Walter on the ground but failed to clear the door. Avarice tsked and shouted at them. "Be careful fools. He won't be of much use if you break him now."

They moaned and grumbled in reply. Walter groaned along with them when they dragged him across the gravel. I winced again.

Avarice ducked inside her limo and waited in the darkened space. The goons dragged me inside and sat down with me sandwiched between them.

"Comfy." I breathed then elbowed the goon on the left. "Give me some room, will ya?"

He scooted closer and smirked.

Boss took out a small silver case, opened it and extracted a long cigarette. She placed it in her mouth, snapped her fingers and lit it with the flame at the end of her fingertips.

With a long drag on the cigarette, she savored the inhaled essences for a minute then exhaled. The silver tendrils of smoke snaked around her face and billowed upwards to the ceiling of the limo. Avarice leaned back, her green eyes on the opened door and waited.

Walter's bloodied form was flung onto the floor of the limo before the doors were slammed shut. Outside the zombies let out cries for brains as they sunk back into the ground to travel back to headquarters. Yup, zombies moved underground. They're faster that way.

Movement rumbled under our feet as the limo went into drive. Walter moaned and bled on the white carpet. A red stain grew around where his head rested.

Avarice tapped her cigarette on the side ashtray and took another puff. Her hooded eyelids relayed her sordid pleasure as the nicotine hit her system. I wiggled in my seat as I felt drops of sweat slide down my backside and soak into the cotton t-shirt.

My movement caught her attention. She blew out the smoke and smiled. "Oh yes, that's right. We have unfinished business to take care of tonight."

"I don't want to be a zombie," I whimpered.

She stabbed the unfinished cigarette into the ashtray and twisted it to snuff it out completely.

"Not my problem," she replied with a shrug. "You knew the price and yet you chose to risk it anyway."

"Uh, can we talk things out?" I licked my lips then hastily added, "Please?"

Her wry smile grew and almost touched her eyes. She crossed her legs and leaned forward onto her arms. I squirmed to free one of my hands and arms loose to rake it through my dirty hair. Should've listened to my brother and done my makeup because I could have been a pretty zombie instead of one that looked like it rolled out of the gutter.

"You have nothing else to bargain with Sarah. Walter's mine along with all of your assets that you once shared with him. What could you possibly offer me that I'd even consider letting you go?"

My eyes shifted from her, to Walter on the floor, who gasped for air, the blood that oozed from his head wounds continued to leak out and stain the neighboring white fibers to a dark crimson.

Would it be so bad if I was a zombie? Thoughts of the decaying slaves and their undaunted reaction to losing limbs like a woman shedding hair sent shudders through me. Yeah, I really didn't want to be a zombie. I'm kind of partial to my limbs for Pete's sake. Oh and living, of course.

Well, when the chips are down it's time to raise the stakes. What I said next would determine my fate. I licked my lips and glanced up with my baby blues to stare right into her greedy green eyes.

"How 'bout a bet?"

CHAPTER
TWO

AVARICE, the Kingpin of Greed, shifted forward as her green eyes lit up with hunger.

"A bet?" he said.

"Yeah, a bet." I leaned my elbow on the goon's meaty thigh and rested my chin on my palm. "If I win, then I go scot-free."

"And Walter?"

"What about him?"

A deep throated laugh bubbled up and out through her lips. She opened her small metal case and snatched another cigarette to smoke. With a light from her fingertip, she inhaled the first puff then blew it out.

"That's what I like about you, Sarah Knight. You don't give a shit about others, and you'll do just about anything to get what you want. It does not resonate with your surname."

"Uh, thanks." I waved the smoke out of my face with my free hand. "So, we got a deal?"

Again, she laughed aloud that shrilled with a high bell tinkle. She took another hit off the cigarette and said, "Hold on. What's the bet, my dear?"

"Ah, right." I rubbed the back of my neck and stared down at Walter's almost still form. He was still breathing but slowing down. His fate was already sealed but I could wiggle my own butt out of this mess. "What if I could raise what I owe you within six months' time?"

"Three weeks," she said and took another drag from her cigarette.

I argued back, "Five months."

"No, three weeks."

"Four months."

"Three weeks."

"Three months."

Avarice chuckled and shook her head, "Fine, you'll have three months to raise the remaining half million that you owe me."

Yes. Should be easy to make that amount within ninety days by doing a bit of hustle and bustle with cards and lucky dice.

"Oh and Sarah." She held up one finger while she took another drag then exhaled. "You didn't really offer me a bet. A new deal, yes. But not a bet. So, to make this an actual bet, you have to raise the funds without gambling."

I paled. Crap.

"I'll know if you step foot in any of my establishments or try anything. Remember, I have eyes everywhere."

Double crap. Right now I was pretty envious of Walter's fate. He wouldn't have to worry about raising such funds in a short amount of time. Where the heck am I going to get that much dough in such a short time?

Avarice clicked a button on the side console and spoke aloud, "Driver, pull over."

"Wait, what?" I gawked. "You're not going to drop me off in town?"

A crease formed in the middle of her brow. "Why should I? That would be going out of my way. I have a tight schedule if I expect to keep Walter. Now, do as I say."

The limo slowed down and pulled off to the side. Gravel crunched under the tires as the vehicle came to a full stop. One of the goons reached over to the door and opened it.

She grabbed my right wrist and the snake slithered back down my arm to its starting position. Red marks were left in its wake. It sat poised above the dice, ready to strike. She smiled and released me. I rubbed the tender areas on my arms.

"Until then, I will reset your mark. You know what will happen if you cross me. Oh, and don't take too long, luv." Avarice curled into a wicked smile.

Avarice nodded towards the opened door that led out to the busy road. "I believe, my dear Sarah, this is where you get off."

"But—" I tried to argue but was shoved out the door by large meaty hands. I face-planted onto the asphalt and spat dirt from my mouth. An oncoming car honked its horn and swerved to avoid hitting me.

The limo was put into gear and drove off, down the road into the night. I got up and ran after the limo. My hands frantically waved at the taillights of the far off limousine.

Walter was gone. Held ransom by Avarice until I made good

on my bet. Part of me missed him. A heavy lump formed in my stomach. I waved again where I last saw the limo. "Bye Walter. I know you'll make a great zombie."

Okay, now which way back to town. I looked right then left and found the stretch of road to divulge nothing of my current location. With a great exhale of breath that plumed before me indicating the chill of the evening air and a roll of my eyes, I held out my thumb, to hitch a ride.

CHAPTER
THREE

THE HIGHWAY at this time of night was sparse. You would think that there would be several vehicles zooming down the road at top speed with no consideration of the various wildlife waiting to spring at some unsuspecting idiot too enthralled with their phone to even see the accident coming their way. Overhead the clouds rumbled and threatened to let loose and drench those below them.

Rain would certainly be welcomed on this hot sticky night. My right arm ached as I held my thumb out at the next oncoming set of lights. I cursed when the stupid car blared its horn at me and continued on down the road. Asshole.

With a breath I blew at my bangs stuck to the side of my face. Yay. Humidity and sweat—a for sure recipe on how to feel disgusted with oneself. I swept my bangs aside and walked a few feet down the road, listening for the next potential mark to come my way.

Backfire sounded before I saw the actual vehicle crest the hill. The old truck rattled and shook down the road. Round headlights shone yellow through the increasing dark evening sky and lit up my dirty clothing. The truck struggled and chugged making other vehicles swerve around it as they sped down on the highway.

I held out my thumb and put on my best dazzling smile even though my hair was plastered to my face with smudges of dirt. The truck slowed down when it approached and stopped. It idled while the driver reached over and wound the window down to talk.

A rush of cool air escaped the truck and caressed my skin. Ahh, bliss. I swooned and took a step closer.

"Evening, miss." A man with a Russian accent, a day's worth of dark scruff on his chin and a cowboy hat said. "Need a ride?"

Cars continued to pass the truck as it idled on the road. I took another step and leaned into the opened window and replied, "If you don't mind."

"Of course not. Get in." He grinned.

My hand reached for the door handle when the old rust bucket of a truck shuddered and let loose a backfire. I leapt back. "Yikes."

A warm chuckle emanated from the driver's seat. "Don't let Betsy scare you. She's just cranky to be out this late at night that's all. Hop in and I'll give you a lift."

Late? At this time? It was barely nine thirty and this bucket of bolts was saying it was late? Ha. My old car would never have objected to a late night ride.

"Well?" he said.

"Sure, sure," I said and opened the door. Another shudder and backfire bellowed out from Betsy. Wow. A temperamental truck. Hmm, wonder if she was by any chance related to Herbie, the Volkswagen Bug.

The guy watched as I fumbled with the seat belt and buckled myself in before he put Betsy into gear and took off down the road. Inside we both sat on a bench seat still with the original cloth velveteen fabric of light beige. Stains of old and cigarette burn holes gave the seat character. In the dash an old A-Track player took center stage but was silent. Her knobs were long gone and only stubs were left in their place. On top of the dash was a beaded mat and a pair of pliers not too far from the radio. Probably used them to tune it since A-Track cassettes went away with the dinosaurs.

From the rear-view mirror hung flashy Mardi-gras beads and a wooden rosary. His work badge also hung from the mirror with the job title, 'Wings of Virtue - Angel On Call.'

I cocked an eyebrow at the driver. He chuckled but kept his eyes on the road and gestured at the badge.

"In case you were worried that I was some sort of killer."

"That badge means nothing, um…"

"Ivan."

"Sarah."

He nodded when I mentioned my name without looking away from the road. He drove slowly. Slower than my grandmother and that was pretty dang slow. People passed him and swore as they went by like their words would encourage Ivan to go faster.

My hands grabbed my knees and scrunched the jean fabric. I jumped back to our conversation by gesturing back at his badge.

"What I meant was that the badge doesn't mean you are or aren't a killer. For all I know is that you are and you prey on unsuspecting hitchhikers."

A grin tugged at the corners of his lips. "Ah, you may have a point. But how do I know that you, yourself are not a killer? Preying on unsuspecting kind samaritans who pick up hitchhikers?"

"Touché."

Ivan's eyes shifted my way but snapped back to the road.

"Mind if I ask, why were you on the road? Kind of late to be out, dah?"

"No, it's never too late." I crossed my arms over my chest and leaned away. "And why I was there is not really your business."

"Ouch." He winced. The sound of the tires on the pavement hummed and were punctuated with Betsy's backfires.

"That tattoo of yours," he motioned with his right hand, "I've seen it before."

"Yeah, so?"

"You seem sweet. Not the kind I'd expect with that type of tattoo."

"Stereotype much? Of course, I wouldn't expect a person like you to have a cowboy hat."

Ivan grimaced and sucked air between his teeth. His left hand gripped the steering wheel tighter. The sound of the leather wrapping creaked and shifted under his hand.

"I mean no offense. But I worry for ladies such as yourselves and wonder how I can help. Remember, that our lord and savior is only a prayer away. Ask and you shall receive."

"Ha." A true belly laugh rippled itself deep from within and continued while I held my sides and allowed myself the silent chuckle. "If only I had a dollar for every time someone said that to me… I'd be rich."

Ivan raised his brows but joined me in laughter. "But it is true."

"Sure, sure." I waved my hand in a dismissive manner. "You keep on believing that then, I'm not going to stop you. I take it that you're a religious man?"

"Dah. Episcopalian."

"Sounds Greek to me."

"We like to joke that we're the fun Catholics without the stick up our asses."

We both laughed.

Signs for the next amenities came into view.

"I can take you to the next gas station. From there I suppose you can call an Uber or a friend to come pick you up."

"Look." I exhaled. "I'm not used to asking strangers for help. Is there any way that you can drive me back to my motel? I don't have any cash on me but I do have some back there. I could pay you back."

He shook his head. "No can do. I've got a partner that I'm picking up. It'll be too cramped for all three of us to ride."

My heart sank. I really needed to get back to the motel to grab my remaining funds.

Ivan frowned. "I'm sorry. I wish I could give you the ride, but part way is better than no way, dah?"

"Sure." I slumped further down in my seat, turned my head to the window and looked out. I couldn't see anything in the dark, but it was better than thinking about my long trek back to the motel. A flash of lightning streaked across the night sky followed by loud thunder.

Rain begun sloshing down against the windshield. Ivan turned on Betsy's wipers that creaked on each passing. The truck slowed down even more to avoid hydroplaning.

I sighed and shifted my weight in the seat. Tonight's walk back was not going to be pleasant.

Ivan reached over and patted my leg. "I will give you funds for the next ride. Least I could do."

CHAPTER
FOUR

WE PULLED into the Love's gas station. The bright yellow lights lit up the numerous stalls. Ivan parked close to pump twenty-eight and turned Betsy off. She protested the change and shuddered and shook to her resting form. Ivan left the keys hanging in the ignition.

He opened his door and maneuvered his long limbs out from under the dash while trying to avoid the steering column. His right knee bumped it on the way out and a hiss of pain escaped his lips. Ivan stood up outside the truck and stretched.

The man must have been at least six foot eight. How he fit into the cramped cabin of Ol'Betsy was a mystery and to be able to handle long rides probably was murder on his back. He rested his hands on his lower back and arched backwards. Once done he leaned back into the truck.

"You can sit for a moment. I have to see if my partner is here.

If not then, maybe I can give you a ride back to your motel. No, promise though."

I nodded and stayed seated.

"Oh, I need to pay for gas too before we pump. Mind Betsy for me?"

Ivan backed out of the cabin, stood back up and closed the door. He rapped the hood as he walked towards the gas station's store. I admired his firm buttocks as he walked away. There was no way that the Lord was looking in my favor tonight. This was too easy.

How trusting was this guy? Walking away while his keys were still in the ignition? The wary side of me was screaming 'It's a trap.' Though the downright scoundrel in me was urging me to borrow the truck instead of walking back to the motel.

Hmm, decisions, decisions.

As I scooted across the bench seat to the driver's side I noticed a brown-skinned woman, clad in a black leather jacket and jeans, dark sunglasses, tight turtleneck and high-heeled black chunky combat boots, walk out of the other door of the gas station. She held a duffle bag on one side and zero'd in on Betsy. With determined steps she crossed the lot in little time and threw her bag into the bed of the truck.

She came up to the window then stepped back. Her wild auburn curls bounced when she took a double-take. The woman lowered her shades, her yellow-amber eyes narrowed while her mouth formed a vicious frown.

"Who the hell are you?"

"Sarah," I replied.

"Where's Ivan?"

"Inside."

"Why'd he leave you with the truck?"

"Dunno." I shrugged and plopped my hands on the steering wheel then reached for the ignition. My left foot pressed the clutch down as I turned the key.

"What the fuck are you doing?" she shouted.

Betsy struggled to turn over. The constant whine of the starter whirled over and over like it couldn't catch a spark. C'mon you stupid truck. Turn over, turn over. It's been years since I drove a stick.

The woman reached in and tried to snatch my hand away from the keys. My left arm moved up to push her back and bar her from entry. Pain bloomed in my forearm and sizzled. Blood oozed from the spot from where the lady bit me.

She bit me. The freaking woman bit me. The urge to stop trying to start the truck was strong. I wanted to jump out and go full on brawl with her. Instead, I backhanded her and she stumbled back just as Betsy roared to life.

With my left foot still on the clutch I shifted Betsy into first gear, pressed on the gas and spun tires. The truck threatened to stall out but first gear caught and hustled me out the stall. Beside the truck the woman ran and tried to hop in the bed.

Oh no, not tonight bitch. I shifted gears again and again to get Betsy moving. The truck rumbled with another roar as she kicked up her speed. The woman's hand came loose from the truck and she stumbled to the ground.

I didn't bother stopping at the road signs and kept Betsy moving. Cars and minivans full of children screeched to a halt as I cut them off and recklessly merged onto the road. Leaving the crazy woman behind us screaming at us. We almost lost traction due to the flooded street.

Ivan stood at the entrance of the store, his bags of goodies fell to the ground, the crazy woman spotted him, stalked over, slapped him and pointed my way. He did nothing but watched me drive off with his beloved Betsy. I guess Ivan was right, ask and you shall receive.

Sorry Ivan.

Betsy threw in a few backfires to punctuate her protests of being stolen and for being driven faster than she normally would have gone. I didn't care. All I cared about was not walking in the rain. Which still was coming down in buckets. My left hand turned on the windshield wipers that creaked on each pass.

Blood trickled down my arm from the bite wound. Who the hell bit people? I thought only toddlers did that? I swiped at the blood and smeared it along my ruined shirt. Guess, I'll clean that up once I get back to the motel too. I hope the wound didn't get infected.

Now, where the heck was I? Which way was it back to the motel? Betsy shuddered. The gas gauge was dangerously close to empty. Whoops. Maybe I should have waited for Ivan to fill her up first.

A sign came up and I spied the familiar logo of the motel on the next exit. I could only hope that it was the same one. I patted Betsy on the dash and said, "Well, girl it's just you and me. I'll show you how to really live."

She backfired in response.

"I'll take that as an enthusiastic yes," I said aloud.

The rain let up to a light drizzle, leaving the road less flooded.

Time to get a move on. I quirked my lips into a smug smile, shifted Betsy into a high gear and slammed the gas. She jerked for a moment and hustled down the road like an old lady rushing to the front of the room to grab her winnings on BINGO night.

Next exit was the motel. Let's hope it was the right one.

RED and blue lights flashed in the night as I pulled into the motel's parking lot. There was a big gathering of cops and people outside my room looking at the wreckage of the door that lay in pieces on the ground. Yellow tape cordoned the area off from nosy motel patrons.

The purveyor of this fine establishment, who sported a rather large gut, was hopping, pointing and screaming his head off. His chubby face had a dark hue, with glasses skewed, from all the yelling and jumping. Spittle flew from his mouth while he spoke and landed on the poor officer's cheek who was tasked to get the details from him. The other cops stood there, nodded their heads and acted like there was nothing wrong.

Betsy took this moment to backfire and announced I was lurking in the darker part of the lot. Heads turned my way, and I slumped further down in the seat. No luck. Gravel crunched under the approaching footsteps near the truck.

A knock on the window sounded. Slowly, I peered over at the person who waited outside the door. He motioned for me to open the window. I opened it a crack and replied, "Evening officer."

"Evening miss. Mind telling me where you were earlier this evening?"

"Out." There was no way I was going to tell him where I was or give more details than I had given him. When speaking with law officials the less you told them the better you were for they would use everything against you. Period.

He frowned and leaned against the truck. The cop let out a dramatic sigh and said, "It'd be easier if you'd tell me where you were—"

"Why the hell does it matter to you." I spied his name tag in the dim parking lot lights, "Officer Jones? For all you know I could be a new customer and you're just scaring me off."

"New customers don't lurk in the shadows. And you seem guilty."

Crap. An officer with brains.

"I'm not," I said.

He peered into the back of the truck and looked back at me with one eyebrow raised.

The cop pointed towards the item in question. "Yours?"

I glanced back, saw the high-quality duffle bag and turned around. "Does it matter?"

"Maybe," Officer Jones replied.

More footsteps and this time accompanied with loud squawks. The motel owner shuffled towards Officer Jones who was questioning me and said, "Quit scaring off my customers you lazy good for nothing cop. I need you to find out who vandalized that room and—"

He stopped mid-sentence when he turned and saw me behind the wheel. If the guy was not super angry before he was now. His face turned several shades darker as he began to froth from the mouth. The owner lifted his finger and pointed at me. "You."

My mouth pressed into a firm line. This was not working out in my favor. Guess karma had been working overtime to deliver my comeuppance.

Going with the cool and unperturbed route I schooled my facial expressions then lounged back and placed my arm on the back of the seat.

"Hello, Teddy."

"Don't Teddy me, you, you—tramp."

"Aw, and here I thought you cared. You even went to the trouble of calling out the calvary when I was mysteriously hijacked from my own room."

He crossed his chubby arms and huffed. "I didn't do that for you. I'll have you know that the cost to fix what your *friends* did is not cheap. I need the police report so my insurance will pay for the damages."

"It was only a door Teddy." I tried to reason with him. A door should not cost an arm and a leg. Especially the low-quality kind that Teddy used in his establishments.

"No, you dingbat. There's a lot more damage than the stupid door. Where were you?"

I set my jaw. "Out."

"Well, do you have any ideas who would ransack your room?" Officer Jones interjected.

Teddy waddled up to the officer and pointed back at the building. "Don't you have some notes to take, officer?"

The cop looked between us and said, "Of course, Mr. Brahm. But don't let this young lady leave. Since that was her room, I have some questions that need answering."

"She's not going anywhere," Teddy replied.

Officer Jones walked away and back towards my rented room.

I hissed at Teddy and narrowed my eyes.

"Why'd you do that?"

Teddy closed the gap between him and the truck and leaned in close to the window. He cupped his hand on the side of his mouth and whispered through the window, "I don't know what the hell Avarice and her goons were looking for in your room but they tore it to shreds. What kind of trouble did you bring my way Sarah?"

"Hey, it's not my fault that the lead about the tattoo specialist you gave Walter tipped the Kingpin of Greed to our location."

Teddy wiped his face with the palm of his hand and grumbled. "Maybe it was your beloved husband that turned on you?"

The absolute thought shocked me to my core. My Walter? Turn on me? Sure his mumsy was not too keen on yours truly but Walter and I loved each other. He'd die for me… but I wouldn't die for him. That's where I drew the line.

Was it possible that Walter was working to double-cross me? Sure, I'd made some mildly inconveniencing bets but we got that worked out. And he never knew that I sold him once or twice until recently. So, it was hardly possible that he was working against me.

"Can you wind the window down Sarah? I'm kind of tired of pressing my face up against the glass."

"But you look so adorable with your pudgy little cheeks pressed against the window."

"Open it or I'll break it."

I held up a hand and replied, "Fine, fine. Give me a moment."

After a few turns of the window crank on the door, I had the window down completely. Teddy removed his glasses and polished them on the ends of his shirt and stared back at the lit room full of cops. He whined.

"Business is going to tank now that we've had a break-in."

I cocked an eyebrow. "Like that's new, Teddy."

He turned his head. "I'll have you know that we hadn't had a break-in in the last eight months. I was kind of proud of that record and here you just had to ruin it for me."

A snort escaped while I laughed quietly. I couldn't help it. When things got tense I would turn to humor to soften the mood. Teddy scowled. The color of his face was a light red. At least he calmed down. A little.

"Look," he said. "All I know is that nothing bad was happening until you showed up. You're like a magnet for disasters."

"Hey." I frowned. "That is totally not true."

Teddy gestured at the motel room and said, "That right there sweetheart, says it is."

"When are those cops leaving? I'd like to go grab my stuff and jet before more disasters befall your fine establishment."

Not to mention I needed to wee. I hadn't had a moment to myself and no, I did not pee while I was waiting on a ride while I hitchhiked. That was a great way of getting a tick up your bum or a spider bite right on the bottom cheeks. Hell, if I wanted a dimple because some brown recluse decided to take his bad day out on me. Nope. So, I'd been holding my wee for a while.

I shifted in the seat and tapped my shoes on the floor. Teddy asked the obvious, "Need to use the facilities?"

My eyebrows lifted, "Can I use yours?"

He chuckled and shook his head no. "Heck, no sweetheart. I'd like to keep my living quarters in one piece, thank you very much."

"But I need to go." I chewed my bottom lip. "Bad."

"Go in the woods."

"What and get chiggers or ticks? Or even bit by a snake or spider? Hell no."

"Well you're not using my bathroom."

I slammed the door open and hopped out. "Screw this. I've gotta go."

With determined power steps I marched to my room.

"Hey," Teddy exclaimed and hustled behind me. "You can't go in there. It's a crime scene now."

I stopped and whirled around on him. He slammed into my chest but took hurried steps to back up. Did I mention that Teddy was short? Yeah, he's short.

He raised his hands and swallowed. "Sorry."

"Teddy, either I go pee in *my* bathroom or yours. Which one will it be? Because I sure as hell am not pissing in the streets or in the damn woods."

The sound of a plastic bottle being crushed not too far away echoed off the pavement as the heavy footsteps behind me approached. A throat cleared and said, "What seems to be the problem here?"

Oh no. Not him. Please Lord, do not let it be him.

CHAPTER
SIX

IF THERE WAS anyone that I most certainly did not want to come face to face with again in the entirety of my life it would be the sleazoid who stood directly behind me. Even his close proximity sent shivers through my entire being. No, not the 'mmm sexy' shivers, I'm talking about the 'heebie jeebies' type of chills.

I felt his hot breath on my ear before he whispered, "I couldn't help but notice that you needed help."

Pee break forgotten I launched myself across the parking lot to stand where Teddy stood who squawked like a chicken to get out of my way. I whirled around, to stare back at the intruder and said, "What the hell are you doing here?"

Tall, dark and ick, dressed in his police uniform, ran his well manicured hands through his hair and let out a tired sigh. He shifted his fit form from one side to the next and pulled out a pack of cigarettes. I watched as he selected one and put the rest away. The cigarette dangled from his firm lips as he fetched the lighter from his pants pocket and then flicked it to life. He pulled the flame close to the cigarette and puffed to activate the addictive chemicals that lay in wait with each cancer stick.

The man took a deep drag, held his breath for a cool minute then exhaled. Smoke intertwined into the night air and gave him a dangerous sexy allure. But I was no idiot. I knew who he was and what he could do to a woman like me.

Though, those cigarettes looked mighty tempting. I reached out. "Can I have one?"

He cocked an eyebrow up. "I thought you quit."

Teddy looked between us and asked, "Didn't you both quit?"

"Can it Teddy. I could use a nic hit right now," I said with a growl.

Teddy crossed his arms and replied, "I thought you needed to pee. Or was that a ploy to get into my suite and rob me blind?"

Oh yeah. I did need to pee. In a mad dash I barreled past both men and the cops into my bathroom. Luckily the door to the almighty toilet was still intact. I slammed it closed and locked it before the cops had a moment to register what had happened.

Though they were banging on it while I was taking care of business. It never failed. You try to go to the bathroom in peace and there was always some jerk that would interrupt you.

"Open up in there," the cops called and banged on the door.

"Give me a minute," I said.

"This is a crime scene, miss and you're messing with its integrity."

I replied, "Don't care. Give me five minutes. I need to freshen up."

"You need to leave, ma'am."

Ma'am? What happened to miss? Was it because they weren't able to cow me out of the bathroom so easily? Nah. Not likely.

"I said give me a gosh darn minute. I'm not a guy so I can't just pee in the woods like you can."

"Fine. You have two more minutes. If you're not out by then, then we'll bust down this door."

Cripes. Was everyone paranoid that I was going to steal this room out from under their noses? True, I did steal a truck earlier this evening, but I highly doubt that I'd be able to pick up a whole building and stuff it down my shirt and walk away. People need to chill.

"One minute," the officer outside the door announced.

I washed my hands in the sink and dried them on the towel then yanked the door open. An officer that was standing in front of the door leapt to one side. Clearly surprised that I finished before his set time limit. I nodded at him and walked out. A set of hands reached around the corner and grabbed my wrist.

"Let me go," I said.

"Sorry, I can't. Since this was your room, we have some questions that you'll need to answer," Officer Jones said.

"Am I under arrest?"

"No."

"Then unhand me." I made a pointed glance down at his hand that wrapped itself around my dainty wrist.

"Can you promise me that you won't run away?"

"I plead the fifth."

"I'll take that as a 'no.'"

Tall, dark and ick entered the room. He narrowed his eyes at the cop who was manhandling my poor arm. The guy moseyed over to where the officer held me in place.

"Let her go," he said with a low growl.

The other cop turned his head, looked him up and down and replied, "Aren't you out of your jurisdiction, Officer Lloyd? You seem to be rather far from the town of New London."

"I was called in," tall, dark and ick said.

Officer Jones frowned, wrinkled his brow before he replied and drew out his response. "Sure."

Tall, dark and ick shifted his feet, set his jaw then leaned down to Officer Jones and whispered in his ear, "Why don't you let this nice young woman go? You don't want to question her tonight. She has not done anything wrong."

It's eerie when you watch others fall under tall, dark and ick's powers. The unsuspecting cop's eyes unfocused as his mouth parted and said, "I do not want to question her tonight. She has not done anything wrong."

Officer Jones let go of my hand then blinked several times. He glanced up and said, "You're free to go ma'am. We're about done anyways."

He moved to the center of the room, clapped his hands and made a circular motion above his head. The other cops stopped what they were doing and waited to hear what the officer in charge had to say.

"Let's wrap up and move on out, guys. Officer Lloyd is taking it on from here. We'll sift through the evidence that we got and compare notes with him later in the morning."

Teddy ran in the room with a cop chasing after him. He bent over to catch his breath. "Wait… just… ah… wait."

Officer Jones peered down at him. The other cop tried to move Teddy out of the room but he refused to budge. He straightened up, pushed his glasses back up and stared right at Officer Jones.

"I need the report tonight." Teddy gestured around the room. "Or my insurance won't pay for the cleanup and repairs."

"You'll get the report in the morning."

"I need it tonight."

Officer Jones pushed past Teddy and clapped his hands again. "Let's move it people."

Teddy reached out and grabbed Officer Jone's shoulder and pulled him back. "I really need that report tonight."

"No insurance company is open this late. You'll get your report in the morning Mr. Brahm. Good night." Officer Jones plucked Teddy's fingers from his shoulder and moved on out the door.

Teddy hung his head and shuffled to the shredded remains of the bed and sat down among the fluff. His hand seized a chunk of bed frame and slung it at the far wall.

"Damn it!" He threw more pieces. Chunks of plaster fell to the floor along with the discarded missiles. "I needed that report. Fat chance those assholes are going to give me the report tomorrow."

Teddy grabbed fistfuls of hair in his hand then hunched over and screamed. "Augh. Fuck me."

Tall, dark and ick was leaning against the wall when he pushed himself away and stepped over to where Teddy sat on the floor. He crouched down and lifted Teddy's chin.

"Easy there sport. I'll cover this mess."

"No thanks." Teddy replied with venom in his voice. "I'd rather eat ramen and ketchup packets for a full year than owe a favor or a debt to your establishment."

"You'll starve."

"Ha! At least I have the reserves to do it."

"Fine, suit yourself. You'll find that the next few months are going to be rather dry for customers and you'll be begging for us to save you from your ramen and ketchup packet fate."

"I doubt it."

Okay, as much fun it was to see these two swing their dicks around it was time for me to get my stuff and leave. The room was trashed. More trashed than when I left it. The poor table and chairs were merely splinters on the floor. Circular spots where the cement was broken and the ground was shifted indicated unwanted visitors were a part of the ransacking activities of this room.

Basically, every single bit of furniture was firewood and other things were torn to bits. It was obvious that they were looking for my trove of goodies but were unable to find them.

What I found funny was that no one cared to look up. I hopped up on the remaining bits of the kitchenette counter and scurried on top of the refrigerator. My hand reached up and around the big exposed pipe and up against the ledge of the wall.

Familiar fabric grazed my fingers and wrapped them around the handle then pulled. My fanny pack popped out from behind the pipes and landed in my lap. I hugged my bag and said, "Ah, there you are... did you miss me, baby?"

Teddy and the other dude had stopped talking long enough

to watch me free my funds from the hiding place. In a flash, Teddy was standing right at the fridge with his hand out.

"You can pay me back for the damages, Sarah."

"To hell I am, Teddy."

He stomped his foot and shouted. "It's your stupid shit that ruined this room. You owe me."

Teddy's face was getting red again. That's when tall, dark and ick seized him and pulled him back. I noticed Teddy's jaw went slack and his eyes unfocused while the guy whispered in his ear.

Tall, dark and ick's voice was too low for me to hear what he told him but I gathered it was for Teddy to leave. For once tall, dark and ick let go, Teddy turned and marched out the door like there was nothing wrong. Leaving me all alone with *him*. I was so screwed.

WITH TEDDY GONE, I had no one to deflect tall, dark and ick's attention from me. He stood there, glanced out the door and ran his fingers through his thick dark hair. I kept on top of the fridge. Not the best of plans but it was one that was working for now.

The guy pulled out his pack of cigarettes again and lit one up. He took a long drag and inhaled the sweet sweet poison then released the glorious second-hand smoke into the air. Tall, dark and ick, certainly made smoking palatable.

A grin split his face as he took another drag, and I scooted forward. I wanted one so bad that I was contemplating forgoing my safe spot just to suck down an unhealthy dose of delicious nicotine.

"Can I have one?" I asked.

He walked away and leaned against the wall, upping the sexy

meter on his whole facade. I knew he was baiting me, but I couldn't help it. Avarice chose her men well and this one did his job beyond expectations.

"Depends." He exhaled another stream of lung choking clouds of chemicals. The cigarette added to the ambience with its own ribbon of smoke. "Are you going to get down to come get it?"

"Um," I said and worried my bottom lip. "No?"

He smirked. "Then the answer is, no, Sarah."

I pouted and batted my eyes at him. "Pretty, please?"

Tall, dark and ick let out a low laugh that vibrated my inner lady bits. He motioned with his hands for me to get down. My cravings for a darn cigarette was going to get me killed and it didn't help that he was sexy to boot.

Don't get me wrong. I still hated the guy and he still sent chills down my spine because of what he could do to people with his powers. Even more so with women who he preyed upon. I swore this guy had incubus in his family line to hold that much sway over people with his suggestive whispers.

He flicked his cigarette to the floor and snuffed it out with his shoe. Once done, he narrowed his eyes at me and said, "Sarah, stop dawdling and get down from there. You have to pay up."

"But this is all I have. I don't have anything else to give Avarice." I hugged my fanny-pack even harder. "And she said I had three months to pay her back."

"I wasn't talking about Avarice's debt."

My stomach bottomed out when I realized whose debt he was talking about. I shifted my legs on top of the fridge and scooted back up against the wall. Tall, dark and ick came closer and reached up to grab my ankle.

"Last chance," he said, "or you're not going to like what happens next."

Warmth began where his hand encircled my ankle and snaked upwards to my center. Everything took on a warm fuzzy feeling that soothed my nerves. I looked down at the guy who held my ankle and felt a surge in my belly. My, was he handsome and strong.

I moved towards the edge of the fridge and reached for his other hand that was waiting for me to grab ahold before he assisted me down to the floor. He still kept contact on my skin which continued the delicious feeling ebbing through my entire being.

With one hand he took my fanny-pack and placed it down behind him and cupped my face with his other hand. We searched each other's eyes before he tilted my head back and went in for a deep sensual kiss. More of the electrical buzz surged through me and I almost melted in his arms. My legs were literally jelly when he pulled away and the only thing that kept me standing was his firm hold around my midsection.

Butterflies were on full flutter while a tiny alarm in the back of my mind was screaming for me to pay attention. Though the rest of me didn't want to listen. This felt good and I wanted more.

"That's better," he said and stroked my cheek. "Now let's talk about how you're going to pay me back for helping you out tonight."

Heat flushed my cheeks and I moaned. "Oh, Vincent."

His other hand began to snake downward while he continued to stroke my cheek. "Shhh. It's okay, Sarah."

I leaned into his hand and enjoyed the warmth. All of it felt so good. But the back of my mind was still shouting that I needed to wake up.

Vincent's left hand unbuttoned the top of my jeans and said, "Let me show you how you can pay me back."

The butterflies in my stomach dropped dead and the icy feeling of betrayal took over. The warm sensation left, and I snapped back to reality. We were leaning on the floor lengthwise close to each other. His hand postured to take the plunge when I rolled away from him.

His eyes turned dark black while a scowl grew upon his lips. I jumped up and buttoned my pants and said, "Not today Vinny. Not today."

Vincent snarled and leapt to his feet snatching my fanny-pack from the ground. I tried to grab it from his hands but he turned away and yanked the zipper free. His meaty paws were about to extract the stack of cash from my bag. I couldn't let him do that.

With his back turned to me I did the next best thing that came to mind. I grabbed the cabinet door that laid on the ground and whacked him over the head with it. The door snapped in half once it made contact with Vincent's noggin. He paused long enough to turn around then fainted.

The stack of cash scattered to the floor. I yanked my purse out of his hands and took handfuls of the bills that I could stuff into my fanny-pack. Why the heck did he undo the bindings? It wasn't like he was going to leave me with anything.

Vincent groaned and was about to come to, by the time I

collected most of the bills back into my bag. Last thing I wanted to be was to be here when he woke up. Vincent was a person you did not mess with and unfortunately, I was already on his shit list before tonight. Let's just say that the last time he tried his mojo on me I kicked him hard in the jewels and left him curled in the fetal position of a casino lobby.

"Sarah." He mumbled while he rubbed the back of his head. "Get back here."

"No can do, Vinny. I've got a hot bet to deal with. You understand, right?"

"Get. Back. Here. Now," he growled.

"I'd love to stay but I've gotta run." I made kissy sounds, blew a few kisses his way, waved goodbye and said, "Ta-ta."

As I rushed to Betsy, and tried to not slip on the wet ground, I heard Vincent roar my name. Chills traveled up and down my spine as I fumbled with the door and hopped in. My hands shook as I worked the ignition and tried to get Betsy to start.

She whined and whined and sputtered. My left leg began to weaken as I held the clutch down. In the doorway of my old room stood Vincent, his form shown dark, with the light of the room pouring out around him. He roared again and marched towards Betsy and me.

"Come on, come on, you stupid truck. Do you want to be scrapped? Because if you do not start, right now… YOU. WILL. BE. SCRAPS," I said to Betsy while I tried to get her to start.

When Vincent was halfway across the parking lot, Betsy roared to life, and I shifted her hastily into first, then second gear. She lurched and jerked across the pavement and squealed tires as we sped past an angry Vincent.

We managed to get out on the road when Vincent yelled, "You're not getting away from me that easily Sarah. You owe me and I will collect what's mine."

I shifted gears, stomped on the gas and left him behind in the dirt.

CHAPTER
EIGHT

THE DUFFLE BAG in the back had tumbled to the tailgate and was visible in the rearview mirror. That crazy woman had left it there. Well, she really didn't because she thought Ivan was in the driver's seat and not little old me. So, she had no intention of getting her belongings stolen.

I promised myself that I'd look in it at the next stop we took which would probably be a gas station because Betsy was on 'E'. There were probably some items I could sell for cash but not until I took care of Betsy first. Scary men with sexy super powers notwithstanding, a stop at the gas station had to happen, regardless of my current situation with the supernatural underground mafia, unless I wanted to walk again.

While I focused on the road ahead an obnoxious jangle started to play. I searched around the cabin looking for the offending object but could not find it. The song started again and I determined that it was a phone but it was not out in the open.

So, either the phone was under the seat or it was in the glove box.

I looked in the rearview and gambled that Vincent would not show up during the small window that I'd take to pull over to the side of the road and look for the phone. Though I did consider popping open the glove box to see but that would require coordination that yours truly did not possess in great quantities.

Betsy shuddered when I shifted her into lower gear and guided her off onto the side of the road. Her tires crunched the gravel underneath and flattened the tall grass as she came to a stop. The phone rang again, and I left Betsy idling in neutral while I flung the glove box open.

Nothing but maps, old air fresheners and some condoms. Ivan seemed like the type to be prepared for any occasion. I bet the ladies loved him. The phone continued to ring and I searched with my hands under the seat but found nothing.

Adventurous as I was, I decided to stick my hands between the cushions to find the errant device that teased and beckoned me to discover its hiding place. As I searched, I felt a smooth and sleek profile wedged between the cushions of the top and bottom near the middle of the bench seat. It slipped from my grasp a few times like it enjoyed the game of chase.

Irritation frayed the edges of my nerves when I pulled the blasted thing out. It was silent for a moment and then blared to life with the annoying song of *Peanut-butter & Jelly Time*. Who in their right mind chose that song for a ringtone? I answered the call with a low growl, "What?"

"Good. I thought you had half a brain for a moment there and had chucked Ivan's phone out the window when you stole his truck. Now that I know you still have it I want you to know that I will find you and make you pay for your treachery," said the crazy woman from the previous gas station.

"Get in line," I said then ended the call and chucked the phone out the window onto the road where it got crushed by an oncoming car. The plastic, glass and technical bits were scattered everywhere. Try and track that, crazy lady.

I still felt queasy as my stomach rolled into somersaults. Crap in a hat. How could I be so foolish to not check for phones? They probably knew exactly where I was at this moment. And it wasn't just them, I also had Vincent the crazy sex demon after me.

Well, I certainly did not have time to sit here on my thumbs and wait for either crazy lady or Vincent to hunt me down. I shifted Betsy into gear and merged back into the stream of traffic on the road. Betsy sputtered when I changed gears and almost stalled out on the road. I glanced down at the gas gauge and groaned. We really needed to stop or Betsy was going to just stall out completely.

The next exit was close and it sported at least three gas stations. If I was lucky then we would make it and get out of here before the calvary found me. Betsy shuddered and groaned as I pushed her past her normal driving speed but I needed her to get a move on for time was not on our side.

We turned off at the next exit and crawled to the nearest gas station from the exit. As we rolled into the station and got close to a pump, Betsy stalled out. She ran out of gas just as we touched down. My arms worked the steering wheel, unpowered, to make sure that we didn't hit the pump as we rolled to a stop.

I got out to pump gas and stifled a scream. The input for the tank was on the other side. Ugh. There was no way I could move this hunk of metal and steer her to a new pump on the right side. Okay, it wasn't time to panic. There was a solution and I only needed to stop and figure it out.

Betsy needed gas. A little bit would allow her to start up and then I could move her around to the correct side so that I could finish filling her up. But how?

I stood there tapping my chin when an older man, with big bushy white eyebrows that threatened to cover his eyes, came out of the station and said with a whistle, "Seems you've got yer self in somewhat of a pickle, miss."

"Err, yeah," I replied.

"Didn't quite make it, did ya?"

"Nope." I grimaced, then asked, "Got a solution?"

He rocked on his feet and hung his thumbs in his pant's belt loops and replied, "I sure do."

"Enlighten me."

"Well, if you get some gas in yer truck then you'd be able to turn her on, right?"

"I was thinking that—"

"But ya don't know how to get that gas in her if she's facing the wrong way."

"Go on."

"Ya got a gas can on ya?"

Like, I said. I would have figured that solution out, eventually. I glanced in the back of Betsy. The duffle bag was there but no gas can. With a shake of my head at the man, I said, "Nope."

"No worries. Ya can borrow mine. Come on in and I'll get ya set up so ya can get on yer way."

He hobbled back into the station, and I snagged my fanny-pack first before I followed him in. Inside the station was what you'd normally expect of a station. Fluorescent lights overhead were bright and shown down on the products below. Shelves held oodles of goodies like chips, cookies, candy and more.

The man motioned for me to follow him over to another aisle and disappeared from view. I hustled over to where I last saw him and he popped back up with a small gas can in his hands. He turned and smiled at me.

"Ya really shouldn't be without a gas can when you travel on these roads. Regardless of yer car's age. T'aint safe at all. No sir-ee."

He shoved the can into my arms and hobbled a few more feet and grabbed a few more roadside emergency things that he thought that a woman like me should have while traveling. I raised my brow as the load in my arm got bigger. I stopped.

"Hey, sir, I know you're just helping and all but I only need the gas can and some gas."

The man stopped, frowned and scratched the scruff on the side of his face before he replied, "Oh."

"No offense." I have no idea why I was being nice to the guy. Guess it was because he genuinely wanted to help me out. I placed the unwanted items on the shelf next to me and went to the front and waited.

He hobbled to the front and took his spot behind the counter to ring up my purchase. I paid for one gallon of gas and went outside to fill it up. Hopefully, Betsy only needed a gallon of gas to get started up again.

After I transferred the gallon into Betsy's tank on the other side of the pump, I hopped back into the truck and started her up. She whined a few times but did turn over with a few backfires to protest being used this late at night. I maneuvered her over to another pump and made sure I was on the correct side. Satisfied I turned her off and went back into the station to pay for more gas.

"Nine gallons on pump two." I plunked down the money needed that would ensure I could put more miles between my pursuers. The old guy was on the phone but rang me up. He threw in a bag of chips and a cold soda on the house then winked.

I waved and thanked him for the food and help then left the station. Thirst won out over hunger and I opened the cool bottle and drank half of it down before I even made it to Betsy. Another pee break was in order later on down the road if I kept on drinking this much soda.

While I sat in the driver's seat I had one more problem. I had no idea of where I was going nor had any inkling of how I would make good on my bet since gambling was not allowed. Maybe one of Ivan's maps may give me a clue?

I opened the glove box and snagged the map for Georgia. With the map unraveled and spread over the seat I took a look at all the places that he had circled. There were a lot of them. Some of the places he marked had symbols, almost angelic symbols, marked near them.

What I needed was a place that had people but not so busy that I'd be up against some fierce competition for my hustle. My eyes snapped to one location that Ivan had circled in bold lines. No secret scripts were written around it, but it kept on pulling my attention.

New London.

I had heard of it and from what I remembered it wasn't that far from Stone Mountain. It was a budding town with lots of new commerce being built. Plenty of opportunities for swindling and making good on my bet.

Though, if Ivan had circled this town, should I even risk going there? Or should I pick somewhere else? No, I felt drawn to this place. I needed to be there. If Ivan and crazy lady showed up then so be it, I'll just give him his truck back. No harm, no foul. I'm sure he'd understand, right?

I put the map away and started Betsy up again. She purred like she knew my intentions. I patted the dash and said, "Alright, Betsy, it's just you and me. Let's see what kind of trouble we can get into in New London, shall we?"

She backfired in agreement and we sped down the road towards New London.

CHAPTER
NINE

HAVE you ever really wondered about the homeless? I mean really wondered about them? How they got there? Why they continued to live their lives scraping together a few measly dollars for their next hot meal or perhaps to indulge their addictive habits? Ever asked one to tell you their story? And did you ever wonder if some of them were true?

These were the questions I asked myself every time I donned my beggar's outfit to cull a few dollars out of unsuspecting bleeding hearts. I took inventory to ensure I had the costume ready for showtime. Falling apart shoes, check. No expensive watches, check. Clothes, simple gray hoodie and sweat-pants with several rips and holes from crazy lady's duffle bag, that looked like they've been soaked in human juices for the past few months, courteously of moi, with unhealthy aromas, check. It still surprised me that the crazy woman from the gas station had these clothes. The other items in the duffle bag were intriguing as well and would fetch me a hefty sum when I visited the local pawn shop.

Next step was my hair, and to rub dirt all over my body. I did not have to do much because I was still smudged with grit from the night before. My hair needed to be more grungy. In the sink of the motel room, I made a paste with Georgia red clay, moss and water. Then slathered it into my blonde hair and massaged it in to make it super dirty. I had to look convincing to get people to open up their purse strings.

My eyes had heavy bags and dark circles under them because I had yet to sleep. Which worked in my favor because some homeless people do look tired… that or super crazy. I didn't have the energy to act nuts this time around. Maybe next time.

Betsy and I had made it to the budding town of New London in the afternoon. Just in time for rush hour on their most traveled road that had all of the new businesses and attractions. I kept my eyes out to see where people flocked to the most and kept note of it.

With the trusty notes in hand, and cash hidden in my sweatpants, I scrawled a short sob story on a piece of cardboard that I found in the trashcan near the front office of the motel. Then I headed out the door and walked to the first location that had a lot of foot traffic.

Rule number one of begging, do not drive to your location. If you can, walk. The moment someone sees you pull off in your expensive luxury vehicle consider your cover blown. You will not make another cent once you've been made.

Rule number two, don't forget to remove all jewelry, watches and expensive clothing. I do not care if those cushy sole inserts are prescribed for your feet or back. Leave them behind. Homeless have only what they can scrounge up and they will wear what they have until it literally falls off of them.

Rule number three, do not harass the people. Unless you choose to do the crazy act then do not pour on the sob story to people. It's a good way of getting the cops to take notice of your residence in the area and a quicker way of killing your hustle.

I settled on a bench close to a trash can in the small park that was nestled between the stores of the new shopping area not too far from my motel. With the sign in my lap I sat back and put on the sad puppy-dog eye look. Several people glanced at my sign but turned their heads away like they didn't see me and sped up to get away quickly. Those were not my marks so I took no offense.

More yelled at me for being a lazy son-of-a-gun and told me to get a job. Yet, again, those too were not my mark. For them, I calmly looked behind them like a cat does to a human, which caused the verbal assaulters to get uncomfortable and leave.

Yet, some people slowed down, read the sign and let out a comforting remark before they placed a twenty, fifty or even a one-hundred dollar bill in my hand which I stuffed into the front pouch of my hoodie. However, these people, as kind as they were, were not truly my mark either.

The day pulled into late evening when my mark finally came to me. He oozed money and compassion as he approached me with a hanky held close to his nose.

"My gods Barbara. Will you come look at this?" He swayed his hand at me, but I kept still and waited. A woman in a black uniform approached from behind him, several bags in her hands and wrinkled her nose.

Barbara cocked her head to one side and replied, "So? She seems content to be here in the park. You do not need any more strays sir."

"But she needs me," he said and inhaled more air through his hanky. "Just look at the poor thing. Her hair is a mess, and god only knows when she last took a bath in clean water. For all we know she showers under a sewer grate."

"Sir," Barbara narrowed her eyes but continued, "what if she isn't truly homeless?"

Uh-oh. Seems like Barbara was wise to the ol'homeless guise that many used to earn some fast cash. Or it could be that her boss had been burned by too many of us in the past. Either way I did my best to not let on that I knew that she knew or it was game over.

"Oh come on Barbara. You're such a stick in the mud." The guy came closer and Barbara tensed. "Let's take her home and wash her up."

"No," Barbara said. "I'm sorry sir but the answer is no. You told me to keep you from making the same mistake and well sir, this is me keeping my promise to you."

So, someone had pulled a fast-one on this man once before… interesting.

He made a high pitched sound and his eyes became wet and glistened in the lamp lights that were turning on in the fading sunlight. The man replied, "But she needs our help. I feel that she genuinely needs our help. Not like that last sod."

Barbara pressed her lips into a firm line and clenched her

fists. The bags rustled amongst each other in her hands. She glared in my direction like her gaze would make me turn into dust and she wouldn't have to continue her fight with her employer.

He stepped between us and crouched down to look me in the eyes. I gazed back into his hazel eyes filled with compassion. The man truly did care and wanted to help. His hand grabbed my sign and pulled it free of my hands. He read it over and over as though several more read-throughs would absolve the hurt that I had supposedly endured in my so-called down-on-luck life.

"Charles." Barbara blushed, turned her head to one side but stepped forward. "I mean, Mr. H. Leave her be. It's getting late and we really should be going. If she's here tomorrow then we'll do something."

The man, apparently, Charles, caressed my cardboard sign then sighed. He said, "Why do you always have to be right, Barbara?"

"Because I am a woman, sir." She grinned back at him.

Charles handed my sign back, reached into his back pocket and pulled out his wallet. He pulled out a wad of cash, shoved it into my hands and said, "I might not be able to take you back with me sweetheart. But I know there's a nice motel not too far from here that you can get a nice hot bath and get clean. You'd like that, right?"

I nodded. He was referring to the motel that I was already staying at. Hell if I was going to speak and break the spell of this charming knight coming to the rescue in the form of moolah. He turned to Barbara and said, "Hey, give me the outfit that Chelsey was going to wear. This poor gal needs it more than her."

"But sir," Barbara began.

Charles wagged his finger and replied, "I'll hear nothing of it. Just drop the bag over here and then we'll be on our way."

He sauntered off a few feet as Barbara came up and dropped the bag with more force than was necessary at my feet. She bent forward and said in a low whisper, "You're all alike. If it wasn't for me, my poor boss would be a true penniless person out in the ravages of our unkind world. People like you make me sick."

Barbara spat at me then turned away. Charles winced when he noticed Barbara's uncouth behavior. He said, "Sorry about that. Chin up, stay safe and things will get better."

He certainly was an odd man. I waited until the two bundled themselves into an upper-end luxury car and zoomed out of the parking lot. My hand still clenched tight around the bills he gave me before he left.

I stuffed the cash that I earned from simply sitting on a bench in a park all day in the bag that had what was once Chelsey's outfit along with the stack of cash from Charles. There were fewer people milling around and prime time for me to leave. It was only getting darker and becoming prime time for real predators to start prowling around. Also, if I stayed any longer then the cops would get wary of my lurking in the park and come harass me. After last night I had no incentive to get their attention.

Upon leaving the park I heard the squeal of brakes right behind me. My name screeched loudly so that all patrons in the shopping area stopped and stared our way. Part of me wanted to book it but that would make my presence in the area even more suspicious.

So, I paused and turned around. My stomach quelled and my throat ran dry. I swallowed a hard lump when I recognized the person behind the wheel of the car. Yet, another person that I really did not want to see again. It was Walter's mother.

The witch sat there in the driver's seat with her dark hair piled high in a hairspray beehive. Her bright crimson lips pulled in a long line and scowl. She revved the car like she was going to run me over. Good thing I went pee earlier otherwise I would have wet myself.

CHAPTER
TEN

WALTER'S MOTHER sat in her expensive sports car and revved the engine. The amount of times that she did it made me think she was not going to do it. Not with so many witnesses around, anyways. I lifted my hand and did a small wave and said, "Hi Glenda."

She shouted out the window. "Don't you 'Hi' me you hussy. Where's my boy? Where's my Walter?"

Crap. Walter's mom was clingier than a dryer sheet stuck inside of a sweater. Or clingier than white animal fur on a black top. His mother literally smothered him with her constant hovering and daily if not hourly calls. Since Walter was currently being held hostage by Avarice it only made sense his mother would seek me out.

Oh, and the small fact that I totally forgot that she lived in New London. There was a high chance that I would have run into her while I did my hustles for cash. The car revved longer and got louder.

I shouted back at her, "Keep doing that and you're going to destroy that car's engine."

"Tell me where Walter is," she growled and emphasized with another rev of the engine. "Or I will splatter your guts on the pavement in front of everyone."

"I'd like to see you try," I said and crossed my arms over my chest as I took a strong stance in front of the vehicle. People around us began to murmur. Some were already filming our exchange. Aware that we were about to be made the hot topic of most social medias I approached the wicked witch's window.

"Look, we can't continue our talk here. People are probably already posting our stand-off online. Can I meet you somewhere?"

Glenda's scowl deepened. Her long ruby red nails clacked against the steering wheel as she thought of her next response. She motioned her head to the passenger side and said, "Get in."

I hopped over to the other side, opened the door and sat down. She wrinkled her nose and said, "Heavens, you smell horrible."

"That's all part of the charm." I winked and reached for my seatbelt.

She huffed. "Well you better damn well hope you don't stain my seats. Or there will be hell to pay."

Glenda did not wait for me to buckle in before she tore down the small travel way in the parking lot and cut several people off. She laid on the horn a few times and flipped the bird. It was a miracle that she had not been in an accident or been the target of some angry idiot with road rage that outmatched hers.

She pulled into the local cafe's parking lot and snatched the parking space close to the front while cutting off the other car that clearly had the right of way. One glare from her made the person in the other vehicle shrink down in their seat and continue down the lot to find another spot. Glenda turned off her sporty stead and sat in silence.

The only sound was her nails tapping on the side of the wheel. Her face was in a permanent sneer while she sat there carefully contemplating her next words. Not wanting to wait for her any longer I unbuckled my belt and opened the door. The movement broke her brooding spell and she followed my lead.

I waltzed over to the door, with my ill-gotten goodies in hand, and held the door open for Glenda with my free hand. She passed me without even muttering a thank-you. I didn't feel like fighting her over the slight and followed her inside.

Dim lights set the mood of the local cafe as smooth jazz played over the speakers. Patrons were scattered throughout the room and sat at the tables. Most were students working through their fifth evening cup of joe while they whirled their fingers over name-brand laptops to get whatever papers that were due the next day or possibly later this evening done. Procrastination at its finest.

I found Glenda snapping at the poor cashier who requested that she repeat her complex order at a slower rate so that he could make sure it was done right. Her fine manicured nail jabbed the countertop on each word as she said, "I should not have to repeat myself young man. My order is easy. You just were not listening."

"You're right ma'am. I'm sorry but would you please humor me? I only want to make sure I got your order right."

"Only because you said please," Glenda said with a wicked smile. I wanted to punch her and then pummel her to paste when she repeated her gawd awful complex order at top speed. The poor cashier was sweating by the time he finished writing down her order. He swallowed like a large lump was stuck in his throat when it was time for him to repeat her difficult order.

"That is wrong," Glenda screamed. "How can you not get this simple order down?"

"I'm sorry." He hung his head.

Oh for Pete's sake. I shoved myself between Glenda and the cashier and said, "Two tall lattes, please."

He grimaced and faced Glenda. Her eyes threw daggers my way, but I was used to her vicious attitude. I said over my shoulder at Glenda, "It is two tall lattes, right?"

Her smile faded and turned into the normal scowl that she wore and replied, "Fine. Two tall lattes, and don't skimp on the foam."

The lad nodded and rang us up. Glenda and I walked to the side to wait on our drinks when the guy said, "Go ahead and take a seat. We'll bring them right out to you. Okay?"

I bobbed my head and replied, "Sure."

"No, I'll—" Glenda tried to protest but I took her hand and dragged her to one of the empty tables. We both sat down and did not bother looking at one another. She continued to sniff and wave her hand in front.

"For heaven's sake, Sarah. Did you have to make your costume so convincing?"

"It does the job. Skimp on the attire and you don't make as much. Odor is part of adding to the believability that I've lived without."

"Well," she huffed. "You stink."

"Yup." I agreed. It was a fact that I could not refute. This meeting might have been more comfortable if Glenda had given me a moment to go clean up. But apparently the knowledge of where her precious Walter was trumped both of our olfactory senses.

Our lattes came out and the guy made sure that Glenda's had foam that peaked well beyond the rim of the cup. She smiled at the mountainous delight and used her finger to scoop out a savory bite. Glenda closed her eyes and sucked the sweet froth off of her finger.

I took a swig of my delectable brew and let the energizing go-go juice send tingles throughout my entire being. It was a few moments before Glenda asked, "Where is my son?"

"Like where is he right now? Or where did I see him last?"

She sipped her latte. "Don't play games with me. Where is he?"

"With Avarice."

"Why?"

"Dunno," I lied and took another swig of my drink then peered out into the dimly lit room. People sat in huddles with their study groups or friend outings. Having a normal life. No knowledge of zombies or other supernatural existence were to interfere with their everyday lives. How I missed being normal.

"Sarah, I know you're lying. Tell me the truth or I will run your soggy ass over with my car. Witnesses or not."

I sighed but kept my gaze centered on the far table in the room. Nothing special about it. I did not want to face Glenda when I told her where her son was at this very moment.

"He's with Avarice."

She inhaled with a sharp gasp. "Again?"

I ducked my head and waited for her to hit me. It never came. She always hit me. But not this time.

Instead, a low sob escaped her mouth and she placed her arms on the table and buried her head. She said in a soft voice, "I told him that you were no good for him. I told him you'd be the end of him. Why didn't he listen to me."

Her hand pounded the table with each iteration of 'why didn't he listen to me.'

"Because, love is blind," I said in a whisper.

The mascara around her blue eyes streamed down her face when she looked up. Her crying ruined her finely tuned visage. She sniffled and wiped away the snot with her sleeve and sat back up. I offered her a napkin to dab some of the mascara away while she fixed her makeup.

When Glenda finished resetting her appearance she glared my way that froze my entire being. Her well manicured talons tapped on the well worn tabletop as she spoke.

"You will help get my son back," she said with a growl and added, "And you will divorce him so he will never be your bargaining chip ever again."

Glenda took a moment to stare at my reset tattoo and

motioned at it. "By your reset tattoo that means you have bargained with Avarice for a new deal. I have a better one."

"I can't go back on my deal," I replied.

She leaned in and showed her teeth with rather long canines. "You will or I will make you regret your choice."

Right. Half werewolf. Totally forgot. Don't ask me how that works. All I know is that she did not become furry like a normal werewolf, and you didn't want to piss this woman off when the full moon came round which by the way was in two days.

"Fine. I'm listening." I motioned for her to continue.

"There is an artifact that I know that Avarice has been hunting. I used to own it but it was swindled from me a few years ago from an old friend of mine. You will retrieve it."

"And that's it? How does that save your son and absolve my debt? Or what if I decide to give the artifact to Avarice myself?"

Glenda took the last pull on her drink and slammed the paper cup down on the table. "My you're not too bright are you, my child?"

"Enlighten me."

"If you try to double cross me then I will hunt you down and kill you. So, don't even try it."

"Okay." I sipped the dregs of my drink.

"You give me the artifact. I hand it to Avarice who then gives me back my son and I then pay Avarice what you owe her. Though, you will then owe me but that's better than being owned by her."

"And the tattoo? How do we stop it from reactivating and enacting the kiss of death?"

Glenda shrugged. "Not my problem. You know how long it

takes for the snake to slither up your arm. And since it has been reset I estimate you probably have two or three days to make good on my offer."

I scrunched up my face. That did not make any sense. Avarice said that I had three months to pay back my debt. Why would I only have three days to make the money back? I decided to voice my confusion.

"That timeline doesn't track. Avarice and I agreed on three months. Not three days. What would she get out of me dying after those three days were up?"

Glenda's blue eyes turned gold for a half second and back to the crystalline blue. She bared her teeth once more and replied, "Two zombies, instead of one."

Crap. That did make a whole lot of sense. It made sense because Avarice didn't care if I paid her back. She didn't want someone who had already betrayed her running around and making more trouble for her. And she probably sent Vincent on my trail to slow my ass down.

Double crap. I pulled out the cash that I had gathered tonight and begun counting it. With Charles' contribution it came to six hundred even. A drop in the bucket considering how much I owed Avarice.

I turned to Glenda who watched me like a cat watches a mouse. My hands grabbed my knees and scrunched the sweat-pants fabric. She had a point. It was either work with my mother-in-law or become a zombie.

Being the anti-zombie enthusiast that I was, I asked, "Now, where is this artifact?"

CHAPTER
ELEVEN

GLENDA HAD DROPPED me off at the motel after we went through the finer details of her deal. I was to obtain this old camera that would somehow help me obtain the artifact that she needed for her bargain with Avarice. Though, I highly doubted that the camera would even be useful.

I showered and rinsed the gunk out of my hair. The hot water sluiced over my alabaster skin and sent the dirt down the drain. It felt good. Much better than the other motel with the weak water pressure. I used the bottles of shampoo and conditioner in my hair and lathered up with the bar of soap to get squeaky clean.

Once done, I turned off the water and grabbed a soft fluffy towel from the rack and wrapped my body in its comforting allure. I grabbed another towel and twisted it around my head for my wet hair. The bathroom mirror was fogged up with the condensation of the hot shower. No matter, I didn't need to look at myself in the mirror to brush my teeth anyways.

While brushing, I considered my next move. Glenda had said that the mark was an old woman with a generic last name, Mrs. Smith, who was looking for a photographer and a videographer to take photos and videos while she talked about her history. She wanted to have something to leave her family to remember her by when she moved on from this life.

It was times like these that I wished for a laptop; however, Walter warned me when we escaped that they could track us with our technology so we had to leave it all behind. Including our phones. I missed my smartphone. The clamshell burner phone that Glenda gave me could only do simple text messages. It did not have the capabilities to surf the internet. Thus, I was left to depend on the information given to me by my mother-in-law.

My gut twisted thinking that I had been had. That no matter which way I went, I was trapped and there was no way out that didn't end with a dramatic death or being zombified. I exited the bathroom and walked over to the bed where the outfit that was once meant for Chelsey was laid out. The dark colors of the garments were not too drab but they would not have been something I would have chosen myself. Though, beggars could not be choosy.

The black slacks were tight and I hadn't even buttoned them yet. Maybe I needed to lay off the creme pies and candies. I sucked my belly in as I snapped the top two buttons before I exhaled. The waist still pinched and was uncomfortable. Unfortunately, I did not have any other pants to wear unless I wanted to dig into my funds and buy some that would fit. The blouse billowed in its dark crimson affair and fit perfectly.

No socks came with the outfit but there were a pair of two-inch black chunky heels to finish off the assembly. Breathing was not comfortable due to the ill-fitting pants. I decided to buy some that fit and maybe an outfit for the next day too. Especially if Glenda made good on her word about paying off my debt in exchange for my divorcing her son Walter. Yeah, I definitely needed to go get some new pants that fit, soon for I couldn't keep sucking in my gut.

On the other bed in my room I had all the items from the crazy lady's duffle bag laid out. She unfortunately did not have any extra pants either. Only the sweat pants, which I ruined for the costume. The rest of the space was taken up by various weapons.

Weapons that a normal person would find odd to have in a duffle bag. However, I did not even blink twice at the bundle of wooden stakes, canteen of holy water, hand-held crossbows, garlic grenades, several pieces of silver in various forms and more. I knew that most of this stuff could be pawned and the pawnshop that I was to visit was known to purchase such items.

I glanced at the time and shucked off the clothing and set my alarm for early am. I had already wasted one day so I needed to hustle tomorrow to get in and out with the artifact. The snake tattoo on my arm was still in the same place that it was yesterday. Which was puzzling.

If the tattoo only had a three day time limit then would it not have already traveled part way up my arm? Who was telling the truth? I mean sure Avarice could have shorted me the agreed time but if that was the case then wouldn't the tattoo have moved?

I shook my head. Unless, Glenda was wrong. She had a sense of urgency about her but that could have been the effects of the full moon coming about too. And she did get fussy when her darling son didn't call her back. Ugh, I couldn't figure this out running on no sleep for the past twenty-four hours.

What I needed was a good night's rest. In the morning the facts would be clearer. After making sure that the door to the room was locked, I shoved a chair under the doorknob. Not that it really helped but it made me feel more secure. That and I was on the second floor so it was less likely I'd get unwelcome visitors during the night.

The lights were turned off except for the one by the side of the bed. I turned down the thick comforter and fell into its soft embrace. Another check on the time set for the alarm, I turned off the light and closed my eyes. Sleep found me immediately.

CHAPTER
TWELVE

AN ANNOYING CHIRP jolted me from slumber. It took me a moment to realize where the heck the chirping sound was coming from, which was the clamshell phone on the dresser across the room. Why was it there instead of the bedside? I guess I must have left it there when I undressed for bed.

The phone continued to cry aloud for attention until I gave in or it got tired. When it stopped there was only a moment of reprieve before the phone started chirping again. I threw the covers and stomped over to it.

"Oh for the love of," I said in a loud voice and added, "What?"

"Dilly-dallying dear?" Glenda's voice purred. "You should already be up and out the door. My sources say that there's competition for that old camera. Chop-chop."

I glanced at the alarm clock and scowled. "It's freaking five am. What pawn shop is open at this hour?"

"One that serves the supernatural, dearie."

An involuntary shudder went through my body. The way she said 'dearie' reminded me of the Big Bad Wolf in Little Red Riding Hood. Was it smart to put all my eggs in this basket and bank on her saving my ass? Probably not.

"You better get a move on, dearie."

"Fine. Fine," I muttered and ended the call by snapping the phone shut. Curse that woman and interrupting my beloved sleep. I shuffled over to the alarm clock and turned off the wake-up call scheduled for later on this morning. Then I shambled over to the clothes and put them on.

Oof. The pants barely fit. How could someone naturally fit into these without needing a torture device or be considered human? Chelsey was probably not human.

The phone buzzed and I took a look to see a new text message from Glenda.

"Did you go back to sleep? Get moving."

I scrunched my face up and darted my eyes to the left. Either she was being impatient or she was spying on me somehow. Most probably magic as it had been ever since Walter turned my world upside down. How I wished I could go back and be normal again. Ignorant of the supernatural world and all their creatures that went bump in the night.

After I stuffed everything that I wanted to pawn into the duffle bag and the rest of my stuff in a plastic bag, I hustled out the door and locked it behind me. Started up Betsy and drove a few hundred feet to the front office to check out. Better to not stay in one place too long considering I had a sex demon and a few others hunting me down.

Betsy and I puttered down the almost clear highway and turned down the lonely road that led to the pawn shop with their lights on. The other establishments on this street were dark. Only the pawn shop was open for business.

No other vehicles were here. I turned into the closest parking lot and turned Betsy off. She only backfired once. Guess she was happier with my treatment or maybe I drove her better than Ivan ever did. Meh. I shrugged, grabbed the duffle bag from the seat beside me and went into the shop.

The bell above the door rang with a cheery chime. There should be a law against being this cheery. Everything should be dull until noon, at least for me.

I approached the counter and hefted the duffle bag on top then glanced at the goodies within the glass case. Five minutes after I entered the store, a man with a bald head, rather husky, came through a door from the back room. His blue eyes were full of cheer and wonder when he came over to me.

"Oh, hey. You're not Ivan," he said then asked in a bright tone, "What can I do for you?"

Swiping sleep from my eyes I replied, "No, I'm not. First, I have stuff to pawn and second, I need to know if you have a specific camera."

"Camera? I have lots of cameras. Are you looking for a DSLR? I have plenty of those if you want to take a look."

I shook my head. "I'm looking for something more vintage."

"Ah," he replied. He motioned at the bag. "Before we go looking at my collection of film cameras, let's take a look at the goodies you've brought me."

"Fine," I said then opened up the duffle bag and laid the

objects out on the counter. The man observed while he also watched the door. Was he expecting Ivan? Could it have been the same Ivan? I exhaled to calm my nerves. No need to get all worked up on what-ifs with no clue of what might happen.

I placed the bundle of wood stakes on the counter and said, "Okay. Ready when you are chief."

He snapped his head back my way and let out a whistle at the arsenal of weapons and ammo that were arrayed on his counter-top. His hand scratched the bottom of his chin as he perused the items that lay waiting for an offer.

"I've got enough wooden stakes and I don't need any more silver bullets. But these," he hefted the hand-sized crossbows in each hand, admiring the handiwork, "these I can give you something."

"Like how much?" I arched an eyebrow.

He smirked and put them back on the counter. "The best I can do for you is two-fifty."

Seriously? That's his best? I had to resist the urge to call him out on his Pawn Star fanboy-ism. I countered his offer, "Fifteen hundred."

"Three hundred."

"Twelve-fifty."

"Lady, you've gotta be kidding me. Five hundred."

I crossed my arms and stepped back. "Eleven hundred."

"Five-fifty."

"Bull. I know those are worth more than that. One thousand."

He nodded. "True, but you're not going to get top dollar. I've got to make a profit. Six hundred and that's my final offer."

"Sold."

The bell to the shop chimed along with a familiar voice. I snapped my gaze over to her.

"Dawson, do you still have that camera?" she said.

It was the crazy lady from the gas station. Clad in leather, bad-ass wrap around sunglasses and boots. She shucked out of her black leather coat and folded it over her arms and was busy stomping the dirt out of her shoes. When she looked up her mouth popped open.

Her surprise was short-lived before she stormed over to the counter.

"Just what the hell are you doing, Dawson?" She snatched the crossbows from him and gathered her things back into the duffle bag. "These are my things. Not this whacko over here."

"Uhh," he replied. "I'm sorry?"

"Sorry my ass. You have done some stupid things in your life and this by far makes the damn list. Why the fuck did you not notice the monogram on the duffle bag? Or the symbols?" she chided him.

"Sorry, I didn't get a real close look at the bag." He rubbed the back of his head.

"Bullshit. You knew exactly whose weapons this bitch had and you were eager to get your grimy paws on them. Shame on you Dawson. Shame."

While the two were tossing words around I sidled to the other side of the room to get away from the crazy lady whose name was still unknown. What was interesting was that she didn't even consider me being here since Betsy was parked out front.

The woman turned on me and pointed. "And where the fuck

are you going? Don't think you can just waltz on out of here with Ivan's truck again. I want his keys, right the fuck now."

She motioned with her fingers for me to come forth and place them into her hands. Since I still needed to get a camera I might as well play along. I reached into my tight back pants pockets and drew out Betsy's keys and tossed them to the lady. Like lightning she snatched them out of the air and pocketed them before I even had the chance to blink.

"You can go now." She shooed me with her hands and turned back to Dawson. "Now, about that camera."

"DSLR?" Dawson asked.

The woman leaned on the counter with her hands and bared her teeth. "No, dipshit. You know which one I'm talking about."

I spoke up, "Wait, Dawson, you were going to show me some cameras too."

Dark brows arched above the woman's dark sunglasses before she sneered. "Dawson's busy."

"I was here first." I jutted my jaw out and walked towards the counter. "So, Dawson, show me the vintage cameras."

Dawson looked between us and said, "Ladies, please."

"Shut up Dawson." We both shouted then continued our staring match. The tension in the room became fierce. Like a cat fight was about to break if a sudden sound or movement happened. Dawson walked backwards, slowly, so that he could go retrieve the cameras.

While he was gone I decided to be somewhat civil. "Name's Sarah. You?"

"Mary." She flexed her fingers. "I'm still considering

whooping your ass for what you pulled back at the gas station and for trying to sell my stuff."

"I would do the same," I agreed, taking a less hostile stance and leaning against the counter.

Mary followed my example and leaned back as well. We both heard rustling and boxes tumble in the back room along with loud cursing. Dawson burst out of the back room with a net wrapped around his foot. He shambled to the counter and put the box of cameras down for Mary and I to peruse.

During our search we set aside cameras that we were not interested in. Only two left in the box. We reached in and grabbed for a camera. Ours landed on the same one. Well, this was awkward.

CHAPTER
THIRTEEN

"OH, HELL NO," Mary quipped with long drawn out vowels then tugged hard on the camera. I tugged back. "Let go!"

"Nope," I replied.

Dawson kept quiet during our fight. He waited for the victor of this fight to discuss the price of the camera. Mary pulled on the camera but I kept a firm grasp on it. This was the camera that Glenda told me about and was needed for today's gig. Why on earth did Mary need it?

Another yank followed by Mary who said in a low growl, "I will not let SUM minion waltz in here and take what is rightfully mine."

"Hey. I resent that. I'm not some minion."

She showed me her teeth and motioned at my tattoo. "Not some. *SUM.*"

"Huh?" My brows scrunched lower, and I let go of the camera. Mary snatched it close to her chest like a bejeweled prize far too precious of unworthy onlookers. She placed the old thing on the counter and turned to Dawson.

Before she had a moment to speak, I asked and motioned with air quotes, "What is 'some'?"

Mary cocked her head to one side and peeled her upper lip away like I was some smear on the floor that had the audacity to speak to her. Dawson looked like he wanted to answer my question but Mary held up her hand for him to be silent. She even did several shushes when he tried to protest. If we had ever met on different terms I felt like we could have been friends.

"You've never heard your people called that?" She gestured to my tattoo. I shook my head and waited for her to continue. Mary let out a sigh and massaged the bridge of her nose before the brow. "How long have you been with them?"

"Eight, eight long years."

Her hand dropped from her forehead to her side and her lower jaw fell open. Either my time with the underground mafia was a good thing or a bad thing. I was leaning towards bad because of Mary's current reaction. Even Dawson stood there dumbstruck. No one moved in the shop.

"Why? Is that a problem?" I asked. I was genuinely curious because of their reactions and wanted to know their take on it. Not like I could truly hide my association with the tattoo blazoned on my wrist for all to see. And no, I wouldn't wear long sleeves to hide the tattoo. The weather was hot and sticky down here in the south. The heck, if I was to wear long sleeves in this dreadful heat.

"The problem is, you slow-witted wet rag, you should know the acronym, S-U-M, for the party that you yourself serve. After eight years you should know who and what *SUM* is when people mention it."

I'll admit that I did hear that name thrown around but I'd always assumed they'd said the word 'some' and not '*SUM*.' I still had no idea what it stood for in regards to the supernatural underground mafia. At that moment a lightbulb went off in my head followed by the smack of my palm on my forehead. I shook my head in my hands.

Mary grinned and leaned on the counter. A warm chuckle escaped her lips. "Seems like our dimwit is not so dim anymore."

"Ugh," I replied. "How did I not catch *that* until now?"

"Dunno, don't care." Mary turned her head to Dawson and nodded at the camera. "How much?"

"Trade one of your hand-held crossbows for it?" His eyes sparkled at the potential deal. "I'll throw in the two whole warehouse boxes of 35mm film if you give me the pair."

"Oh hell no," Mary said. "Do I look stupid? Did I come in here with stupid painted on my forehead or something? If you want stupid then try dummy over there but not with this camera."

"Fine. Fine," Dawson said and added, "One thousand."

"Fifty," Mary countered.

I jumped in with my bid, "Two hundred."

Mary arched an eyebrow and replied, "You ain't part of this negotiation, dimwit. Butt out."

Dawson shifted his eyes between us. He said, "Nine-fifty."

"Dawson, you're trying my patience today. I won't let you get first dibs on my next raid if you keep this shit up. One-hundred for this piece-of-junk camera that ain't worth more than fifty."

"I can give you five-hundred for it, Dawson," I said. Dawson wanted to take my offer. He clearly wanted to scoop the five-hundred and call me the victor of the camera, but I could see it in his eyes that he was also terrified of Mary and the clout that she carried. If he crossed her then the possibility of interesting wares in his shop would come to a screeching halt.

Mary strutted up to me. Her hips swayed with each step. She placed her hand on my chest and pushed me back slightly, leaned in and said, "I said, butt out, dummy."

This woman was strong. She did not back down for nothing, and I could tell she wanted this camera but did not want to pay through the nose for it. Mary pivoted her back towards me and moved to her original spot at the counter to continue her bargaining with Dawson. The two fought on the price. Part of me wanted to add to the swirl. Only part of me? Well, okay, all of me.

I took a step closer to Mary and Dawson to butt in once again when I saw a green flash come from the box that held the other camera. I stopped and looked down into the box. The other camera laid there, it had no flash of its own and the shutter button was not depressed or anything. So, what flashed?

Carefully, I scooped the camera out of the box and examined it. My left hand pulled the napkin out of my other back pocket to look at the sketch of the camera that Glenda wanted me to purchase. This camera did not match the drawing. The vintage camera in Mary's hand matched the sketch. Though, when I held this camera in my hand it felt warm, and I felt it call to me.

The supposed cover job was a photographer to take pictures, so, that meant this camera would work, right? It was unlikely that I needed the exact camera that the other woman was so enraptured with and doing her best to pull the price down to something that wasn't gutting her wallet or purse.

With a shrug I held up the camera and asked, "Dawson, how much do you want for this camera?"

He froze. Mary stopped talking. Dawson motioned with his hands for me to lower the camera and said, "You don't want that camera."

"Why not?"

"It's cursed. That's why."

"Cursed?" I arched an eyebrow. "How?"

He swallowed and pulled at the shirt collar around his neck. Dawson whispered, "Everyone who has owned it has ended up dead within a week's time. The damn thing keeps on coming back here."

"Seriously?"

Mary butted in, "Yeah, seriously, Dawson? You put *that* cursed thing in with the others? What were you thinking, you fool?"

He threw her a look and replied, "I thought *you* were going to take that damn cursed thing off my hands today. Guess I was wrong."

"You bet your ass you were wrong," she quipped.

Dawson inhaled deep and let it out in a shuddering breath. He looked back at me and motioned at the camera and towards the box.

"Yeah. So, put that one back. Choose another one."

The camera pulsed in my hands. I could feel tingles ooze

through my limbs and the call. Like a siren, I felt compelled to keep this camera. My grip tightened and I said, "No."

"But, it's cursed," Dawson balked. "I can't have your death on my conscience."

"It's my life," I argued. "If this camera ends me then it was meant to be. Not your fault."

"I can't," he grimaced. "Please, choose something else."

"Nope."

"Fine. Make me an offer."

"What? You're not going to haggle? What if I say twenty-five cents? Are you going to accept that with no fuss?"

He grabbed a box from under the counter and put tissue paper in it. He then grabbed utility leather gloves and put them on. Dawson plucked the camera from my hands and placed it into the box. He held out his other hand and said, "That'll be twenty-five cents, please."

No freaking way. This guy has got to be nuts if he's selling me a camera for twenty-five cents. All because he believed it was cursed. I grabbed a bill from my fanny pack and held it up to him and asked, "Can you break a twenty?"

"No, but we'll consider the rest a handling fee." He snatched the twenty from my hand then shoved the box over to my side of the counter. "May the next seven days of your life be all that you've wanted because that camera is going to make sure you won't see day eight. Now leave."

I gathered the box and started towards the door.

Mary said, "It was nice knowing you dimwit. Too bad you aren't long for this earth. At least in eight days everyone's belongings will be safer with you gone."

"Yeah, whatever Mary. Whatever." I waved then stopped when I realized that I had another problem. Since Mary took back Betsy's keys, I had no means of transportation. I turned back and looked at her.

"Hey Mary, can you give me a lift?"

She turned to me and hitched her hip up to one side and laid her fist upon it. She lifted her lip away from her teeth and replied with long drawn out vowels, "Oh, hell no."

FOURTEEN

THE DOOR to the pawn shop slammed behind me. I hunched my shoulders forward expecting additional violence to leap forth from the door. None came. Every hair on the back of my neck was standing up. It wasn't like I was on edge due to the cursed camera that I now had in my possession. No, the feeling was coming from somewhere else.

Mary and Dawson were still within the shop haggling the price of the vintage camera. I looked at the camera in my hands. I was unsure as to why this cursed old thing called to me. Oh well, a camera was a camera. Not like Glenda was going to know that I got the wrong one for the gig. I only needed something that I could point and shoot for photos. That's all.

Now, my other problem might have been transportation but after a few years with the mafia I'd picked up a few tricks that were rather handy in these types of situations. I shambled over to

Betsy and thanked my lucky stars that I did not lock her doors otherwise this would have been a lot harder.

Reaching under the steering column I removed the shield and exposed the wires. I placed on the bench seat the box that held the cursed camera. The hairs on the back of my neck were still raised which made the next part rather unnerving. I had this sinking feeling that Mary was going to burst out the shop doors and catch me while I was liberating Betsy from her clutches.

With a sneaking glance over the dash, I scanned the area and then went back under the wheel to find the wires that I needed to hot wire the truck. There was a mass of wires but only one with black electrical tape around them. Obviously, this wasn't the first time that Betsy was hot wired.

I unwound the black tape when the ground on my right shifted. Yup, that would explain the unease that I felt when I walked out here.

His voice rasped when he said, "Hello Sarah."

My head hit the underside of the dash and I turned. Which gave me a better view of the undesired visitor. The khakis and shoes were still rather new. Only recently made zombies possessed such attire. Older zombies had shredded rags or roamed naked showing off their sun worn jerky skin. Gross.

I sat down and smiled at him. "Hey Walter. Long time no see."

"Bullshit. You did this to me." He gestured to his newly dead form with clothing from the other night stained with blood. "So, how are you going to undo it?"

"I'm working on it."

"How do I know you're not just running away?"

Pointing to the snake tattoo, "Because this thing will make sure I follow through or I'll be right where you are now."

"There's no way you'll make good on your new deal. Avarice has set you up to fail."

"You don't know that. I've pulled my ass out of the fire several times in the past."

"Yeah, with my help."

"Well, I got help," I admitted. "And I'll have you unzombified before you can say *'braaaiiins…'"*

His dead eyes, slowly turning milky white, stared deep into my soul and he asked, "Who?"

I turned back to working on getting Betsy started with no keys. My fingers got zapped each time I crossed the wires. Ouch. Walter leaned in, the smell of his flesh wafted into the cabin and rolled over my nose. I gagged.

"Walter, don't take this the wrong way but man you reek. You don't look bad, but you could put on some cologne to cover up, you know, the dead smell."

"I'll take that into consideration. Now quit dodging my question and answer me, who is helping you?"

"I can't tell you." I tried the wires again. Betsy whined and threatened to backfire. I shushed her and replied back, "If I tell you then Avarice will know."

"Like she wouldn't know already," he said.

"Fine. I'm working with your dear old mumsy. Happy?" Betsy whirred again with the promise of starting but threw a loud bang. I hope they didn't hear that in the shop.

Gravel crunched under Walter's shoes. He didn't breath but still hovered like he wanted to tell me something. Finally, he inhaled and said, "My mother is not to be trusted. She is far better at using and disposing people than you are my dear. If you can get the money another way then do it. Don't fall for her trap."

"Honestly Walter, do you think I'm that stupid? As of right now your dear mummy has the better choice for the both of us. I get this artifact for her, she gives it to Avarice to free you and your dear ol mummy has agreed to pay off my debt to Avarice as well."

His eyes narrowed to slits. I guess zombies could do that and he was freshly made. He asked, "Why would mother agree to pay your debt?"

With a wave of my hand I replied, "Because you and I are getting divorced after this whole fiasco."

Walter hissed. I knew he wouldn't like that part of the deal. But a deal's a deal. Another pass with the wires and Betsy turned over. Her engine thrummed in the parking lot as I hopped back into the driver's seat.

Rolling down the driver side window I leaned out and said, "Walter, as much fun as we're having at this reunion I really have to go. I promise to be careful and watch out for your dear mummy's tricks. I've got this. Now be a good boy and report back to Avarice since I know she has you spying on me."

He grumbled and shambled back to his hole. Before he sank back into the ground he said, "Don't trust my mother."

After that he was gone, and the ground had covered itself back up. Betsy belched another loud bang and the shop door opened. Mary searched the lot and locked her eyes on my back in the driver's seat of Betsy. I waved to her as I pulled out, shifted gears, squealed tires and left her in the dust.

I gave a final salute with my middle finger to her shrinking form as I sped down the road to my next destination. Bye Mary. Hope I don't see your sassy ass in a long while.

CHAPTER
FIFTEEN

NESTLED in the old part of New London where land was plentiful at the town's infancy was an old house that sat way back on many acres. Iron wrought gates barred entry to the grounds and access granted only to those who were invited. On a normal day, yours truly, would not have gained entry. But, today was different, for today, the woman who owned the luxurious estate needed some lowly photographer to take her pictures as she told her life story.

The man at the gatehouse nodded his cap at me and flipped a switch for the gates to roll open. Betsy in a show of appreciation of the kind guard that did not make her wait, fired off a succession of backfires as we rolled on down the pristine drive. Though, I suspected that Betsy looked forward to making her mark on these maculate roadways that led us to the living area in the far back of the property.

I patted her dash and tried to soothe her ire. "Easy Betsy. We're just going to go in and out. That's all. Should be a piece of cake."

Betsy backfired in response. The feeling was mutual for I felt on edge too. Nothing like using a cursed object to win back my life for at least six days before I bit the dirt. But hey, way better than three. Or was that now two? Gah, I couldn't remember.

Another glance at the inert tattoo on my right wrist. The snake was still in its reset position though I could have sworn that I felt it slither up my arm late last night. Yet, that could have been my nerves getting to me once more. If only I could be normal again. No more mafia, zombies, half-werewolves or whatever supernatural I'd dealt with in these past eight years. I would gladly enjoy six days of normalcy if I didn't feel the press of the mafia thumb on my head no more.

The driveway ended in a circular path that led back out. I pulled up in front of the white granite steps and parked Betsy, who of course, belched more backfires in protest of being turned off. I was starting to get a feeling for the ol'girl and noticed that she only made more noise when things got tense or she sensed danger was nearby. So far, the best vehicle I'd stolen yet even if she was old.

I opened the cardboard box next to me on the seat and pulled out the ancient camera. Thirty-five millimeter film went out with the dodos from what I remembered. So, it was hard finding some in the various drug stores that I looked. Most of the employees stood there with scrunched up faces and could only utter, "Huh?" when I asked them if they still sold film. Too bad there wasn't a Wolf Camera store anymore.

Though I did score some film at a random gas station. The guy charged me an arm and leg for them but I had no choice so I paid the man and for the case of oil that was desperately needed. Betsy needed oil. She apparently sprung a leak between the pawnshop and here. And my limited knowledge of vehicles was that they needed that liquid gold or they'd stop working when you needed them the most.

I hopped out and slammed Betsy's door and snagged my bag out of the back. Yes, I did stop and get some clothes. Most importantly, pants that fit an actual human being. And yes, I would count that as the highlight for today. Pants that fit. You just didn't know when you found a pair that hugged your curves but didn't squeeze the life out of your midsection because you forgot to suck your tummy in. Ah, the brutal reality of not being in your twenties anymore.

As I walked up the steps to the tall ornate walnut, I guess, French doors with opulent carvings and stained glass, a man with pale skin stepped outside. He was clad in a dark suit, had tufts of wispy white hair, years of expressions worn into his face and held the door open for me. He said when I passed him and while he closed the doors behind us, "Mrs. Smith has been waiting for you."

The butler motioned towards my bag and then a large table with a marble surface, "If you would deposit your belongings I will make sure they will make it to your room for the evening."

I was still ogling the interior of the foyer when he cleared his throat. "Madam, if you would place your bags and belongings on the table I can then escort you to Mrs. Smith. She has been patiently waiting for your arrival."

"Right." I blinked and placed my bag onto the table but held onto the camera. The slightest thought of abandoning the thing gave me goosebumps. Strange, I know. The butler arched an eyebrow at me when I shook off the sudden shiver that trailed down my spine. Maybe Betsy was right, and I should have not stopped. Or maybe I needed to stop listening to inanimate objects and stop being a wimp.

"Uh, sure. Right," I said and asked, "No introductions?"

The man frowned but replied, "Ah yes. Where are my manners? I am Mr. Gray. And you are Ms. Knight."

Wait, how did he know my name? He noticed my eyes widen with alarm and he added, "A woman called earlier this morning saying that you'd be arriving this afternoon to do the photo session with Mrs. Smith. We had another come earlier that agreed to do the videography. She's here already, so you're the last one to arrive."

"Oh." My mouth kept the little 'o' structure for I was still perturbed by people making appointments without me knowing. Which meant Glenda was very eager to get this artifact back from the old woman. Hmmm, I wondered if I could nullify my debt with Avarice? However, that would leave poor Walter as a zombie, and I did promise I would get him free.

Mr. Gray walked in front of me and nodded his head toward the hallway. I fell in step behind him and he led me down the long hall. The pictures on the wall were from various timelines. Many different faces, except for one. There were a set of eyes that shone like gold, even in black and white, that followed you as you passed them. Creepy.

"If you would, miss." The butler stopped before a room with

opened doors. Conversation drifted out into the hallway as two women continued discussing mundane things like the weather. I passed the man who nodded his head and slightly bowed when I entered the room. I was not prepared for what I saw next.

"Oh, hell no." The woman clad in dark clothing and perched on a white ottoman said in long drawn out vowels. Yup, our good friend Mary was here. And because we had to stop at a bajillion stores looking for 35mm film, Mary got here first. But why? Was she after the same artifact?

Mrs. Smith clucked her tongue and said, "Language, young lady. Language."

Mary took a sip from the delicate teacup in her hand and kept her pinky alight while she drank. She placed it down and replied, "Of course, Mrs. Smith. Pardon my vulgar use of words."

I stood in the doorway and waited to see how things unraveled. Mary gestured towards me and said, "That woman is no good Mrs. Smith. I know her and she'll just mess things up."

"Hey," I replied and took a step into the room. Mrs. Smith sat on her small pea green wingback chair, with a white doily on the back, close to the fireplace, sipping her tea. She glanced up but did not look directly into my eyes. Instead she held her attention at my chin. Gold glimmered on her irises when she spoke, "Don't hover, my dear. Come, sit."

Mrs. Smith gestured to the other open ottoman that was adjacent to her. I shambled over to the spot and sat my butt down on the cushy seat and took liberties with the snacks laid out on the trays before me that were on the table. I snacked on a few finger sandwiches while Mrs. Smith motioned for Mr. Gray to pour me a cup of tea.

After I swallowed a few bites, I said, "It is a pleasure to finally meet you, Mrs. Smith."

The old woman sat back and perched her teacup and saucer on the arm of her chair and smiled. Her eyes darted between Mary and myself like she was waiting for either of us to start something. I kept my big mouth shut, for once.

Mary continued to glare at me. When it was obvious that nothing was going to come of silence Mary cleared her throat and asked, "Mrs. Smith, did you want to start tonight? Or tomorrow morning?"

"Tomorrow morning, my dear," she replied. "If that is alright with Ms. Knight."

My face was full with cucumber sandwiches that I had to hastily chew then swallow before I could reply to Mrs. Smith's inquiry. I awkwardly hacked an answer when a crumb went down the wrong pipe, "Of course."

After I finished hacking up a lung, and Mary gregariously slapped my back, I asked, "Might I ask how many days you'd like me to stay?"

"A week," she replied and frowned. "The details were in the work request."

"Right." I ducked my head in apology and took a swig of tea. "I wanted to make sure. Sometimes employers change the duration of such contracts."

"Oh." Mrs. Smith smiled. She sipped her tea and nibbled on a biscuit *(or cookie if you want to be all American about that stuff. When you have tea a cookie is a biscuit, end of story.)*

The tension from Mary's side of the room was still thick even after she pulverized my poor back when I had the coughing fit and she decided to ask, "Ms. Knight, if you're a professional then why are you doing the photography with an outdated camera? Heaven only knows where you got the film, and if it's any good, but how are you going to get it developed? And ensure the quality is not compromised?"

Mrs. Smith's eyes brightened at the sight of the camera in my hands. I wondered if the cursed camera's deadline was transferrable? Would be nice to not die in six or seven days and enjoy my hard-earned freedom to normalcy.

The old woman asked, "Yes, why do you not use your cell phone? I hear they have better resolution, and you can instantly see if you have to retake the shot."

Okay, time to put my college education to use... well the bit I did learn. I placed the half-eaten biscuit on the plate, sat up and held my knees. I looked at each of them and replied, "Yes, mobile phone cameras are far more superior today, but I will argue that film has that endearing quality that you cannot capture with modern day technology. In regards to development, I will handle developing the photos for I've done it for years and never trusted another company or person to do it for me. It's a matter of extra quality care that I give my customers to ensure they have the best end product. I'm in the business of memories and film is my medium to make it happen."

Loud clapping resounded in the room as Mrs. Smith hopped off her chair and laughed with delight. She said, "Well said my dear. Well said. You may stay. If only everyone had your attitude about vintage items then maybe things would last longer."

Mary looked between us with her jaw dropped. She tried to say something when a young boy about seven or eight entered the room to pick up the serving trays. Mrs. Smith made him stop so that she could introduce him. "Ladies, this is my grandson, Seth. He is staying with me this summer to learn about hard work and that nothing is easily gained without such work."

He took in the room, looked at Mary, then me and finally the camera in my hands. I caught his lingering gaze before he corrected himself. Seth addressed both of us, "It is nice to meet you. If you do not mind I will go ahead and clean away these dishes if you are done. May I?"

I nodded and Mary mimicked my nod. Mrs. Smith kept her eyes on Seth until he left the room with the used dishes and serving trays. Who makes their grandchildren do chores during their summer or treats them like a servant?

Mrs. Smith rose from her seat once more, grabbed her cane, adorned with a golden dragon's head with ruby gems for eyes, and walked towards the door. She stopped and said to Mr. Gray, "Please show these ladies to their rooms. Let them freshen up and rest before we have dinner later tonight."

Mr. Gray nodded and watched as Mrs. Smith toddled off to another part of the house. More likely to go take a nap after all those tea and biscuits that she consumed. I was feeling rather tired myself but I hung back while Mary got up to leave. Still, Mr. Gray waited until I joined them in the hallway before he escorted us up to our rooms.

Mary pulled me close to her and hissed, "What the hell are you doing here?"

"Wouldn't you like to know?" I smirked.

"Yes, I would like to know, damn it. You're playing with fire by coming here," she replied in a low hush.

"I'm here to take pictures. That's all," I replied.

Mary glanced at the camera. "With that cursed thing? You're an idiot if you think you're going to take people's pictures with it. You need to leave."

"Sorry, can't." I held my hands up. "I've got money to make and a deadline to hit. Any money is better than no money."

"Are you fucking serious?" Her bottom jaw set while she arched an eyebrow. Her amber eyes pierced me on the spot. "Whatever this gig is supposed to pay you then I'll double it if you just leave."

Uh. Hmm. Well that's new. If only I knew how much this gig was supposed to pay me. I wonderws if I could get Mary to pay the remaining amount that I owed? Would it seem suspicious to ask that much? Probably would… but…

"Quarter of a mil," I said.

"Quit fucking around," she replied. "I'm serious."

"And I, too, am serious."

"There's no fucking way that this gig would pay you a quarter of a mil."

"Who said it was what the gig was willing to pay me. It's the price tag for you to get rid of me."

Mary tore at a jagged fingernail and ripped it off. "Fuck."

Mr. Gray, oblivious or ignoring our whispered conversation, led us up a less grand stairway and down another hall that held our rooms. He motioned to the first one and said, "Ms. Knight, you will be staying in the canary room. Please note that there is a shared bathroom at the end of the hall. If you need anything then simply pull on the rope and either myself or someone will address your needs."

He turned to Mary, "Ms. Dawn. If you would follow me, please. Your suite is just a few doors down from Ms. Knight."

"One moment, Mr. Gray. I'd like to have a private word with Ms. Knight."

"Of course." He nodded and went down the hall a few feet.

Mary pushed me into my room and onto the bed. She pointed at the camera and in a controlled voice filled with anger brimming to be released, she said, "This is not a game. Yes, you may have had years with *SUM* but it appears they've sheltered you. You should not be here. That camera should not have even entered these grounds. You need to leave. If I were you then I would do just that because…" She stabbed me with her finger. "Things are going to get a whole lot more complicated."

I arched an eyebrow. "Complicated? How? It's only a photo gig. That's all."

"Bullshit." Mary spat. "I know you ain't no photographer. And bravo in pulling the wool over the old lady's eyes. But I know you're here for something else entirely and it's going to get your ass killed."

"Oh like, how is this camera going to kill me in six or seven days? Or like my magical tattoo that might give me the kiss of death tonight? Or is it something else?"

Mary stood up. Her hands rested on her hips as her eyes were lidded halfway. Her lips were pulled away into a grimace. She replied, "Fine. Have it your way. But know that I'm watching you."

She stormed off and slammed the door behind her. I got back

up and dusted myself off. For someone that had only met me a few times she certainly caught on to my intentions fast. What gave me away? Was it me stealing Betsy again that tipped my hand? Either way, she was going to make it way harder for me to search for the artifact with her breathing down my neck.

CHAPTER
SIXTEEN

THE CANARY ROOM, where I was stationed for the night, was bathed in various shades of yellow. Yellow walls, fabrics and furniture added to the ambiance of the room. The four-poster canopy bed had oodles of pillows in different sizes and shapes. I flopped down on the bed face first and enjoyed the fluffy embrace. Ah, bliss.

My bag was placed in a small wingback chair situated by the window with a small table and lamp by it. On the table was a stack of books from well known authors. Many who I had read in the past. I got up and walked over to the chair, moved my bag down and sat down. Picking up a book I flipped to a random page and began reading.

Minutes passed and the sun outside was getting lower when a knock sounded at my door. I replied, "It's open."

Seth opened the door and asked, "I was coming to tell you

that dinner will be delayed by an hour. Until then do you need anything?"

I shook my head and said, "No. I'm all good here."

His gaze caught on the camera and he said, "You might want to put that up for now, Ms. Knight. For safety, of course."

The camera hung from around my neck, and I totally forgot that it was there except for the warm buzz that emanated from it. I looked down and smiled. "Whoops, I totally forgot I was still wearing my camera. Thanks for the heads up, kid."

Seth narrowed his eyes. "I'm not a kid."

He left but closed the door in a quiet fashion.

I got up and stretched my limbs. Sitting in the chair for hours made me stiff. I passed the floor-length mirror that was in the other corner of the room and looked at myself. Probably should clean up before dinner, my hair certainly needed it. The camera around my neck had an eerie glow and it was pulsing.

My hands reached for it, and I felt compelled to bring it up and to look through the viewfinder. Why was everyone so worked up about this camera? Sure it was cursed but still I doubted that anyone else except Mary knew that about the camera.

I stared at my reflection through the viewfinder and placed my finger over the button to take my picture. With a smile, I said, "Cheese." And took my picture.

There was a flash in the room. Everything spun and I felt sick to my stomach. A warm buzz ran up my right arm. The camera dropped from my hands and yanked on the strap around my neck. I pulled on the summons rope then staggered to the bed and fell face first into the cushions.

And the world went dark after that.

I awoke to a wet cold sensation on my forehead. I groaned. "What happened?"

"You fell," Seth replied. "Luckily you didn't crush your camera."

"Mmmf," I said. "Good."

His voice was tense when he said, "Why use that old thing? Why not use your mobile phone instead? Much better than a stupid film camera."

My body felt weak but I managed to crack an eye open. "Hey. Just because it's old doesn't mean it is bad."

"How so?"

"Film has its blessings too and something that digital cannot replicate. That warm feeling or sense of nostalgia. Digital just doesn't have that."

Seth looked towards my room's door, before he leaned closer to me and whispered, "You need to be careful with that camera. I can sense my granny wants it and she may try to steal it. So you better lock that camera up and keep it safe."

A migraine was threatening to take up habitation in my head. I took the cloth from Seth's hand and placed it on my forehead. Then replied, "Kind of rude to be talking about your grandmother that way, isn't it?"

"I'm saying that your camera shouldn't be here," he whispered. "That you're only making things more difficult and it should really be handled by a professional."

He was questioning my abilities to take pictures? A seven year old? Good grief.

I let out another growl and replied with as much sass as I

could muster, "Excuse me, but I will have you know, that I am a professional. I have a minor in photography." I didn't tell him I never finished that degree. "So, I think I know how to handle a film camera. Thank you very much."

"I wasn't questioning your photography abilities. I was questioning your other credentials. You need to be careful and watch what you're doing, or I won't be able to help you next time."

What? What was he talking about? Saving me from what? Oh, right. I did pull on that summons rope before I passed out. Good thing that was there or I might have missed dinner.

Outside the room Mrs. Smith called up the stairs for Seth. He stepped back and held his hands in a stay motion while he kept eye contact. His eyes also shown with gold but with a fiery hue to them. He said, "Stay there. I'll go see what my granny wants. Don't do anything else with that camera, okay?"

"Sure, squirt. Whatever you say." I laid back on the bed and placed the remoistened cloth back on my brows. The migraine was winning, my right arm burned and I didn't have the heart to argue with some seven-year-old kid about the stupid camera.

Seth turned off the lights, padded off and left me in the darkened room to nurse my migraine alone. Downstairs I could hear Mrs. Smith lay into her grandson about dawdling and taking too long to tend to the visitors. That he was needed in the kitchens and if he didn't hurry she'd box his ears.

Wow. His grandmother was a class-a something. Glad, she wasn't my grandmother. Crazy that she treated him more like a slave than a grandchild. Oh well, not my circus, not my monkey. I only needed to find the artifact and get the heck out of here.

That was after my migraine went away which should happen after a brief nap.

I closed my eyes and let the cool sensations of the washcloth over my forehead ease my aching head. Now if I could only get some rest, that'd be great.

BRIGHT SEARING LIGHTS flared and made my migraine worse when Mary barged into the room and turned on the lights. She marched over to the bed's side table and snatched up the camera. Her fist tightened around the strap when she looked my way.

"You need to leave," she said through clenched teeth.

Pinching the bridge of my nose I replied, "Look, I've got a migraine right now. Can you just give it a rest? Please?"

"I heard what he told you."

"Who?"

"Seth."

"And what did you hear?"

"That this camera should never have come here and that his grandmother seeks to take the camera from your possession."

I waved my hand at her to calm down while I still held the bridge of my nose with the other hand. The migraine worsened when Mary grabbed the camera. I asked, "Can you put the camera back down? I'm worried you're going to run off with it."

"Considering what I guess you might have done with this camera, I might."

Sudden cold flashed through my entire being. That sinking sensation grabbed hold and snapped my migraine in two. Mary should not leave with the camera. Intuition was telling me to not let her leave with the camera.

"You can't. It's my camera." I crossed my arms across my chest. "I paid for it, even if the dang thing is cursed and will cost me my life."

"I've met stupid people over the years but Sarah, you are beyond stupid. You have no idea what this camera is or its capabilities."

"Do you?" I fired back. "Thanks to Mrs. Smith, I know, the camera kills its owners within seven days after acquiring it. Not much to it, if you ask me."

Mary frowned and kept her clutches on the camera. "Idiot."

A knock sounded at the door and Mr. Gray stood there in the doorway. "Ladies, dinner is ready. Please follow me downstairs."

"Sure. Give me a minute," I said while I rolled off the bed and landed on the floor. Oof. Going to feel that in the morning. I popped back up and gave two thumbs up and hustled over to the door.

Mary stood there with my camera in her hands, and I asked the room, "Well, are we going to dinner or what?"

The butler bobbed his head and led us down to the dining room on the main floor. While in route I did try to snag the camera back from Mary but she yanked it away from my grasp. I shoved her and she shoved me back. Mr. Gray had to pause until we stopped acting like children before he finished leading us to the dining room.

The size of the dining room was huge, like two small one bedroom houses stuck together, and in the middle was a long table that accommodated over fifty or more dining guests. At the far end sat Mrs. Smith at the head of the table. To her right was her grandson Seth who stood up when we entered the room.

They both had changed into more appropriate attire for dinner. I was still wearing what I wore earlier this afternoon, basic slacks—that fit, a loose flowing dark blue blouse, but no shoes. Those were still upstairs in my room. Besides, it seemed that it was preferred that we did not wear our shoes within the house and we either went barefoot or wore house slippers.

Mary did have time to change her outfit and I only now realized that she'd put on an elegant one-piece of an emerald green that looked good with her skin tone. I would never have pulled off her outfit. She followed Mr. Gray to her seat beside Seth and sat down in the chair that was pulled out for her. Mary placed the camera to the left side of her as she situated the napkin into her lap.

On the other side Mrs. Smith gestured for me to sit down in the seat next to her. Mr. Gray hurried to pull the chair out for me and let me sit before he scooted it back in. Seth sat back down once both of the ladies were seated. At least the kid had some manners when it came to dining etiquette.

Mrs. Smith's eyes landed on the camera but said nothing. She clapped her hands together and dinner began. The servants brought in the first course which was a delicious beef broth to get us started. The next course were the appetizers that consisted mostly of roasted golden potatoes and steamed green beans.

What drove me nuts is that Mary told me to leave with the camera. Even Seth echoed the same sentiment. But here, Mary took the blasted thing from my room and placed it blatantly on the table right in front of the grandmother who supposedly wanted to steal the camera from me.

I stabbed the food on my plate with more force than was needed and threw nasty looks at Mary. She returned the dagger looks and pieced her food as well. Mrs. Smith felt the tension between the two of us and cleared her throat.

"Ladies, I sense there is something going on between the two of you. Will one of you tell me what is going on? And why is the camera here?"

Not wanting to give Mary a chance to spin her web of lies, I went first and said, "My apologies, Mrs. Smith. Mary apparently liked my camera and tried to steal it. She was in the process of trying to steal it from me when Mr. Gray interrupted her to inform us about dinner." I swept my hand around the table in a grandiose fashion. "And so, here we are."

Mary threw a potato at me. "Bitch, that ain't the truth and you know it. That's so far from the truth your pants have gone up in flames."

"Says the thief with the camera." I threw some green beans at her. Many of them landed in her hair. She gasped and her mouth stayed open. Seth chuckled.

Mrs. Smith's stern eyes pinned Seth in his seat when she said, "We do not laugh at such things young man."

He bowed his head and kept his gaze down and replied, "Yes, grandmother."

More potatoes and green beans flew across the table and hit me in the face. The butter bean stuck and slid down my cheek leaving a greasy trail in its wake. Oh, it's on. I grabbed a fist full of food and threw them across the table. Mary grabbed other bits of food and flung them my way. A full on food fight took over dinner's serene setting.

White table cloths, napkins and place settings stained from the cranberry sauce and gravy that were flung around the room. Scraps of potatoes and green beans littered the floor. And Mary and I had food all over our persons when a loud banging rang in the room.

Mrs. Smith stood there with the large food cover and a big spoon at its side. Mary and I stopped, food still fisted in our hands as we both turned towards our host. She used the cover as a large bell to get our attention.

In a stern voice she said, "Ladies, this is not proper behavior. I am appalled by the both of you. In all my years I've never seen two grown women throw food at each other over a small domestic issue. If you wish to continue your employment for the duration of this job I highly suggest that you both apologize to each other and go clean up."

We bowed our heads and apologized to Mrs. Smith and then to each other. Mary scooped up the camera and was about to leave when the old lady stopped her.

"Ms. Dawn, I believe that camera is Ms. Knight's property. Please give it back to her before you leave this room."

Mary grounded her teeth and stomped over to where I stood

at the table. She shoved the camera back into my hands and said, "Here, you should be more careful and keep this in a better spot if you know what I mean."

"Not really, but thanks," I replied, thankful to have the camera back in my hands. A warm sensation covered my entire being. Almost the same buzz you felt when you got the right balance of being drunk enough but not too drunk that you'd end up puking because the world spun too fast.

She lingered. "I'm serious. Keep it safe."

"Okay, mom," I replied. Mary was being cautious about my camera but was being closed lip about why I needed to keep the camera safe or to be careful with it.

Mary rolled her eyes, turned around and stomped out of the dining room. I followed shortly. Mostly because I needed to clean up as well. Mr. Gray was in the lead to show me to another bathroom since Mary occupied the other one. Behind me, after I was out of sight from the dining room, I heard Mrs. Smith ask her grandson, "Are you sure that's the correct one?"

Seth answered, "I'm sure of it, master."

CHAPTER
EIGHTEEN

I DID NOT SLEEP. Not one tiny iota. Each time my eyes drooped I pinched my arms or did pushups to keep my heart pumping. Why?

As much as I hated to admit it but Mary was right. The camera in my possession was in danger. Our employer wanted to steal it from me, and I suspected she might have wanted to do that last night after we went to bed.

There were footsteps that wandered down the hall throughout the night. Several times the person would stop outside my closed door and wait. Though with me jumping around, doing push-ups and making it clear that I was not asleep the unwanted visitor walked away.

Why would anyone in their right minds want a cursed camera? And what about Mary? What happened to the camera that she purchased from the pawnshop? Why did she not have hers here for this week long photo shoot?

As I continued to ponder within my own mind a knock sounded on the door followed by Gray's voice. He said in a low tone, "Ms. Knight, breakfast will be in the front family room. Mrs. Smith has asked me to notify you and Ms. Dawn to be down in fifteen."

The no sleep vapors played a long beep in my head as I tried to process what the butler said through the door.

"Ms. Knight?" he asked.

"Oh, sure, sure, right fifteen minutes. Got it." I hopped up from the floor from where I sat when I wasn't exercising through the night. Grabbed some nearby pants and shimmied into them. "See you down there."

"Of course, Ms. Knight." I listened to his footsteps as they faded down the hallway and stopped before he knocked on Mary's door and relayed the same information.

Well, the butler was not behind the nefarious intentions of stealing said cursed camera from my being last night. The cadence of his footsteps did not match the other ones. Yet, this house did have other staff and one of them could have been the culprit that ensured I did not sleep a wink.

Ugh. Needed to stop worrying about the stupid camera. Maybe it would be a blessing if the camera was stolen? Perhaps, I would not be on the hook for the curse. I shook my head. One could only dream.

Upon passing the floor-length mirror, I worried my bottom lip and looked down at my pants. They were stained from last night, which meant I couldn't wear these after all. Great.

My hand tucked a stray blonde strand behind my ear while I bent over my opened bag in search of a clean top and pants.

Ones that weren't marred with potatoes and buttered garlic sauce green beans.

For an elderly woman, Mrs. Smith was certainly spry for someone of her age. Mary and I had the hardest time keeping up with her as she sprinted throughout the grounds. She led us through the garden maze adorned with twelve foot high boxwood hedges to the center where afternoon tea was set up.

Mary did not have the camera which she purchased from the pawn shop on her person. Of course, Mary wouldn't need a plain camera since she was doing the videography. Instead, she recorded Mrs. Smith as she led us around the property talking about the history and memories attached to each significant place we passed. The old woman had no issues with Mary capturing her image on the phone however whenever I brought up my camera to capture a picture Mrs. Smith would move out of the way or distract us with something else. She was intentionally avoiding having her picture taken by my camera.

Even Mary stepped aside when I brought the camera up to snap a pic. Yes, I knew that Mary obviously had more information on my camera than I did. All I knew was that the camera was cursed and supposedly all previous owners lost their lives seven days after they acquired this artifact. If only I had more time to do research on it. Especially the weird pulsation that I felt whenever I held the camera in my hands.

Mrs. Smith called out, "Ms. Knight, you look like you're about to fall over. Please come, sit and have some tea. I will not have you fainting on my watch. At least, not again."

I turned to see the gleam in her eyes. She probably was

informed by her grandson Seth that he found me passed out in my room yesterday afternoon. Speaking of which, where was he?

I tucked my hair behind my ear and wandered over to the table and pulled out a chair to sit. I asked when I sat, "Where is Seth, your grandson?"

"He's back at the house doing his summer reading and some chores. Can't have him be idle and get into trouble. Have to keep young ones busy," she said in a matter of fact tone while she stirred two lumps of sugar into her tea and took a sip.

Mary was in the other chair and had her phone facing the old woman. She said, "Tell us more about this maze and garden, Mrs. Smith. Who put the landscape together?"

As tired as I was I could not stay seated or else I would have fallen asleep. My feet protested when I stood up. Mrs. Smith motioned for me to sit down again. I replied, "Sorry, I think I'll take some pictures of the grounds while Mary continues the video interview."

Before she had the opportunity to interrupt, I was already around the hedge leading back to the house. It wasn't much of a maze since they had signs with arrows on them that helped you in and out of the hedge maze. I stretched my arms when I exited the maze and walked towards the large bay window from the breakfast nook in the kitchen.

Inside there was movement. I noticed it was Seth who was doing his chores. Dusting and washing the windows. The camera tingled in my left hand, and I brought it up to snap a picture. As I looked through the viewfinder, my breath left me, what I saw was a man with a gorgeous bod. I mean one-hundred percent yummilicious well-toned body with hard muscles that you'd wouldn't mind him bench pressing you with. He had sun-kissed skin, along with dark hair with streaks of blonde giving you the sense of a delicious summer night. He looked directly at me with his smoldering golden eyes with a smattering of fire, stirring the embers deep within me.

The guy pursed his firm luscious lips, blew a kiss at me and winked. My body was ready to melt and pool on the ground from his wanton actions. I must have looked like a fool while I held the camera up to watch the hottie.

"Hey, what are you doing?" Mary said.

I nearly jumped out of my skin and the camera went flying from my hands. It snapped at the end of the strap around my neck and plummeted down and against my belly. Most certainly the splash of cold water that I needed at the moment.

Mary walked up, glanced at the window and asked, "Again, I'm asking what are you doing?"

I rubbed my stomach from where the camera smashed into me. "Taking pictures. Duh."

"Uh, huh." Mary arched an eyebrow and crossed her arms.

"Seriously." I picked up the camera and pointed it at her. "I can take yours, if you want."

She placed her hand on the lens quick as lightning. "Watch it, fool."

I frowned. "Why? Not like it's going to steal your soul or anything."

"You don't know that." She snapped and huffed. "Remember, how I asked you to leave? I meant it. I've been around cursed cameras long enough to know nothing good comes of them. You're playing with fire girl. You should give the camera to me and go."

"Not happening." I said, got into a defensible position. "Why aren't you with Mrs. Smith?"

"Mrs. Smith wants you with us, taking the pictures. She doesn't trust you to be doing your job unsupervised. And I one hundred percent agree with the woman. So, are you coming back or what?"

"Yeah. I guess." I glanced back at the window. Seth stood where the hottie was a minute ago, still dusting and washing windows. There was no way that it was him. Maybe my sleep deprived brain was playing tricks on me. Which was possible or maybe Seth was the hottie after all but how could that be?

"Well, come on." She motioned with her hand and started to head back to the maze.

"Hold up," I said and saw Mary pause in her steps. "I don't think the camera is working right."

She saw that I had it pointed in her direction and stomped my way. "Will you watch where you're pointing that thing? Do you have any idea as to what you're holding?"

"Yes," I deadpanned. "A broken cursed camera."

Mary rolled her eyes. "You are unbelievable. If you're not careful you're going to kill someone with that camera."

"How? Not like taking someone's picture will knock them dead. Besides, I am not joking. I think the camera is messed up," I said. "Take a look at Seth through it and let me know what you see."

Mary snatched the camera from my hands and glowered at me. She brought the viewfinder up to her eye and pointed the camera at the window. I glanced over at the window where Seth continued dusting and occasionally sprayed with cleaner to wipe the windows clean.

Seth looked up at us, stopped cleaning, pocketed the rag and put the duster in his back pocket. He motioned for us to wait then brought his left hand up in a fist, the back-side facing us. A smirk was plastered on the kid's face as he moved his right hand in a cranking motion close to his left. In a mechanical fashion the middle finger on his left raised upwards.

Seth's eyes widened. His mouth dropped open and his right hand slapped the side of his face. His expression was put-on as though he himself was shocked by the outcome of his action. A twinkle in his eye flashed before he busted out laughing.

The camera was shoved back into my hands. The familiar warm buzz enveloped my whole being. Though, what did Mary see? Didn't she see the hottie? My brows creased upwards in confusion.

"Here," Mary said. "Tain't nothing wrong with the camera. Maybe *you* should get your eyes checked instead."

"Wait," I said to ask what she saw but she didn't even stop to listen.

Mary stormed off. Inside, Seth continued to roll with laughter. I couldn't help but laugh along with him. Mary was too uptight, in my opinion. All business and no play. Unlike Seth, who had his priorities right, even at a young age, play hard no matter what you're doing.

He winked at me and blew a kiss before he went back to

dusting and cleaning windows. Cheeky. I liked that, but too young for me. Way too young.

"GLAD TO SEE YOU ENJOYING YOURSELF."

I whirled around to see Walter standing there. His skin appeared waxier than earlier and his hair was less vibrant than before. A pungent odor clung to him like ripened cheese. Ugh. Don't barf.

"Walter," I stammered and half jumped back. My heart was pounding away in my chest. "What are you doing here?"

"Keeping tabs on you, obviously." He gestured around the area and glared towards the window.

Seth was glowering right back at Walter. The two continued the staring match until the boy gathered his things and left the room. Part of me wanted him to stick around. I did not want to be left alone with Walter. Sure, he wasn't at the point of craving for human flesh or brains but you never knew with zombies. Even the best enthralled zombies had tendencies to lapse into their savage mannerisms.

I took another step away from Walter and clutched the camera. Walter caught the moment and cocked his head to one side. He murmured, "And what do you have there?"

"Nothing," I replied and hid the camera behind me. "Just an old camera. That's all."

"Sarah." Walter sighed. "I know you. And I know that's not just an old camera. Do you even know what is in your possession?"

My fingers tightened around the case of the camera. More warm tingles traveled through my limbs giving me the courage to answer Walter.

"Yes," I said. "A cursed camera that will claim my life force before the week is out."

"Idiot," he said with tight lips. "You're proving that you can't function without me."

"Does it matter?" I waved my right hand in front of me. "In a day, I'll be a zombie like you if I don't find the artifact that Glenda has sent me to get so she'll pay my debt and free you from your fate."

"About that." Walter's dead eyes watched me. "You should forget that deal with my mother."

"Why? Once I find this trinket for your mumsy, I'll jet. You'll get unzombified, my debt will be paid and we'll be on some remote beach in Mexico before you can even utter supercal- ifradgilisticexpialidocious. I'm close, I know it."

"Are you? Really?" Walter asked.

"Yes, damn it."

"Who are you trying to convince? Me or you?"

"Come on, Walter," I begged. "Can't you trust me on this? I'll have the trinket to Glenda by tonight and we'll both taste sweet sweet freedom by tomorrow morning. I promise."

My eyes felt wet. I blinked to hold back the tears and felt my stomach tie itself into knots. The thought of failure was on the edges, and I had to push it away.

"Sarah."

"What?"

"Be careful." He sighed then sunk back down into the ground. I looked down at the unsettled dirt and caressed the camera. Another wave of warm tingles rushed through me but I felt even more tired than this morning. I needed a nap.

In my pants pocket I felt my phone buzz. I plucked it out and answered, "Yeah?"

"You've got two hours to get my trinket or else," Glenda snarled into my ear.

Crap.

"Sarah," Glenda growled through the phone. "Do you hear me?"

"Yes," I replied and swallowed the hard lump in my throat. "I thought I had until this evening?"

"Timeline has been shortened, dearie."

"Yes, but why?"

"Don't question me you little snit," Glenda replied. "Get the artifact within the next two hours or consider the deals off."

"Okay, okay," I said. "But can you give me three? I have no idea where she'd keep the artifact."

Through the phone Glenda groaned and I swore I could hear

her eyeballs roll around in her head. I held back my retort while I waited for her to give me more time.

"You have the camera, yes?" she asked.

I winced and replied, "I have a camera."

"A camera?" she said. "Did I hear you right? You said you had *a* camera? But not *the* camera?"

"What difference does it make? I got a camera. The other one was already purchased."

Glenda cursed a string of expletives over the phone and sounded like she threw it across the room. A series of crashes followed the sound of smack and thumps. Her footsteps stomped over to the phone.

"You…" She paused and finished. "Twit."

"Hey—"

Glenda cut me off. "The camera I sent you to get had special powers which would have made this job easier to locate the artifact. And yet, you nitwit self-decided to make an easy task difficult by purchasing the wrong camera."

"I had no idea. You didn't mention why you wanted that specific camera. I thought it was only to pull off the ruse as a photographer," I argued.

Glenda breathed hard into the phone.

"So, do I have that extra hour or not? I'll get the artifact, but I need more time."

More time spanned. If it wasn't for her teeth grinding then I would have thought that Glenda hung up on me and left me to ponder if I had the extra hour or not.

"Glenda?"

"You have three hours," she said and hung up.

CHAPTER
TWENTY

CRAP. I had three hours to find and deliver the artifact that Glenda wanted or our deal was off. On top of that I didn't have the specific camera to help me find said artifact because Mary bought it instead of me. Which would have been a completely different situation if Glenda told me that I needed the camera for more than a photographer facade. Great. Just fucking great.

A quick look around confirmed that Mary had stormed off, probably back to Mrs. Smith who was still in the maze having tea. Two, Seth was no longer washing windows and three Walter was indeed gone. Which meant, I was free to go snooping for the artifact that Glenda needed to bargain for her son's life.

The screen door to the kitchen creaked open. None of the staff were present which made my job easier to sneak back into the house. I had no idea where Gray was at the moment but I'd worry about him later. Need to find the artifact. Why couldn't my cursed camera help? Was the life-stealing of its owner the only power that it had? Hmmpf. Probably.

If I was Mrs. Smith who hoarded magical artifacts where would I keep them? Either my office or library and with the size of this house the old woman most likely had both. I peered into each room that I passed and opened the doors with quiet precision. The house was oddly vacant unless the staff were on another floor which was probably where they were hanging out between their chores and tending to Mrs. Smith's needs.

On the main floor on the right wing of the house, I found an ornate door with a window set in the top half, leading into a darkened room at the end of the hallway. The camera in my hands pulsed and got more intense the closer I got to the room. The door was made with heavy oak stained dark and gridded with window panels. A brightly polished brass old-fashioned knob adorned the door and beckoned for me to turn it.

Using the cloth of my shirt I wrapped the knob with the material and opened the door. The wood hung heavy on the hinges and gave a loud creak into the darkened musty room. I didn't dare turn on the lights else alerting my host or her staff that I was in this room. The door clicked into place when I pushed up to prevent more creaks while I closed it.

Light streamed in through the cracks of pull-down blinds and around heavy curtains. Stacks of papers were piled on the desk, dusty and forgotten. Dust covered everything in this room in a thick film. The carpet underfoot was worn in trails where the person had worn a track from the desk and to the door. The rest of the carpet, which wasn't covered by piles of paper or junk, was still plush. I made sure to watch where I stepped so I would not crash into something.

The room that I walked into appeared to be the library slash office. Evidence of the many books lining the shelves, paperwork littered everywhere, and the heavy desk situated near the back of the room.

Many objects lined the shelves, too. Lots of them were shiny baubles that had no real use but still looked pretty even with dust covering them. Books were also in residence on the shelves and ranged from Archeological history, myths, fairy tales to several editions of encyclopedias.

The chair behind the desk swiveled around and I jumped backwards and toppled over a pile that was on the floor. Things that were precariously stacked tumbled down on top of me. Ow.

A low snicker sounded from the desk. I rubbed my head and picked myself back up from the mess to see who scared the living daylights out of me. His golden eyes glowed while he propped his elbows on the desk with his mouth hidden behind hands and examined me.

"I knew you'd come here, eventually," Seth said.

My heart was still hammering away in my chest, but I said in a strong voice, "What the hell, kid? Do you normally hide and scare the life out of your grandmother's visitors?"

He leaned back in the chair and propped his feet up on the desk. His hands behind his head. A smug grin plastered on his face. "Nope."

"Why are you in here then?" I asked.

"Why are you?" he replied.

I let my jaw stay open. The kid had a point. I closed my jaw, straightened my shirt and said, "I asked you first."

"Doesn't matter." His grin grew wider. "You have to answer me or I'll tell granny that I caught you snooping in her office."

The little brat had me. Either answer his question or let Mrs. Smith know that I was snooping around. A pulse went through me and I remembered the camera in my hand which gave me an idea. I pointed it at him.

"Tell me why you're here or I'll steal your life-force, right here and now."

Seth's eyes grew wide as saucers and he sat up straight. He held that look before he busted out laughing. His hands went to his sides while he continued to laugh.

"Stop laughing." I stepped closer to the desk and pointed the camera closer.

He glanced up and laughed harder before he shoved the camera away.

I frowned. "Will you stop laughing? You're going to get us both in trouble."

Seth wiped tears away from his eyes, his other hand still wrapped around his waist and replied, "Sorry. It's really funny because you have no idea what you have in your hands."

"Obviously," I huffed. "Apparently everyone and their brother knows what this camera is besides me. All I know is that it's cursed and my life is forfeit within five days."

"My granny could help with that." He gestured at the camera.

"No." I yanked the camera away from him. "It's mine."

I felt like gollum when I said that, but I couldn't help it. The thought of parting with the camera sent chills through me.

Seth quirked an eyebrow up. "Are you sure? She might be able to help you with more than your fated death. Granny might even be able to help with your other situation."

I shook my head. "No. Not happening. Besides, what happened to you warning me off?"

"It's too late." He made a face like he licked a sour lemon.

"What do you mean, it's too late?"

"Granny knows you have the camera. Especially when Mary had it on the table during dinner last night."

"So?"

"So, she'll do anything to get that camera."

I rolled my eyes. "Look, why doesn't your sweet old granny wait until I'm dead. Then she can have her turn to be killed within seven days."

"Oh, that won't apply to her," he said and mumbled, "Or you."

I stuck my finger in my ear to clean out the earwax that had built up in them and said, "What?"

He resumed sitting back on the chair with his legs propped up on the desk. His eyes cut to the door before he spoke.

"How 'bout this? I'll tell you how to find what you're looking for in exchange for the camera?"

"No."

"You're on a tight schedule. I can tell. Can you afford missing the deadline?"

I tightened my grip on the camera's case and sighed. "No."

"Then agree to give me the camera in exchange for the item that you're looking for."

For a seven-year-old his vocabulary was rather expansive. It was like I was talking with an adult instead of a child. Could the camera have shown me his true form? I shook my head and clenched my teeth. The camera pulsed once more.

"How do I know that you won't bolt once I give you this camera? And how do I know that you know what I'm looking for or even know where it is in this house?"

"What I do know is that the other woman is also looking for the same artifact as you. She was in here last night with her camera peering through the viewfinder. Pity that it did not show her the artifact."

I looked up. "The artifact is in here? This very room?"

"Of course." He uncrossed his legs and recrossed them on the desk. "My granny keeps all her precious things in this very room."

"And Mary was in here last night? With her camera?"

"Yup." He popped the 'p' at the end.

"Would mine reveal the artifact's location?" I wondered out loud.

Seth gestured around the room. "It wouldn't hurt to try."

I brought the camera up but hesitated. "Wait, I'm not sure it will work. The camera was acting funny earlier. I think it's broken."

"What makes you say that?"

"Earlier when I saw you in the bay window the camera showed you as a grown man." I did my best to not let myself salivate at the memory of the hottie. "Not a seven-year-old boy."

His eyes sparkled. "The camera shows you what it wants you to see. Not everyone can persuade the camera to function properly."

"Great." I sighed. "Again, how can I trust the camera to show me where the artifact is if it isn't willing to work correctly?"

"Give it a shot."

"Fine," I grumbled and pulled the camera up to look through the viewfinder. Immediately the room was ablaze in various lights shimmering off of every object in the room. I brought the camera down to blink, shook my head and took another look.

"Crap," I said and dropped the camera. It yanked at the end of the strap and pummeled my stomach. "How can I find the artifact in this humongous collection?"

"You aren't too bright are you?"

"What?" I snapped my head toward him. "Just because I can't find the artifact among artifacts doesn't mean I'm stupid."

He held up his hands in a placating nature. "Whoa. Easy. Do you remember any details of what you're looking for? Like size? Shape? Color?"

I ran my hand through my hair, sighed and paced the area between the desk and door. "The item is small, made of metal, ornate decorations, and looks like a lamp."

"Okay that's the same description that Mary had written down on some paper in her room."

He was in her room? Why? Okay, I don't need to know. All I need is to get the artifact before she does since Seth told me that she was looking for it too. For once, I'd like to get the upper hand.

"Is it in here?"

"The lamp?"

"Yes." A pause. "Maybe."

"But you said earlier that it was in this room. Were you lying before?"

"Maybe."

Ugh. This kid was so frustrating. Helpful one minute and hindering the next. I pushed my hair back once more and searched through the bookcases for a lamp. Maybe it looked like Genie's lamp from the tale of Aladdin or perhaps it looked like the one from *I Dream of Genie*. More than likely it looked like the one from Aladdin.

One thing Mrs. Smith had going for her collection was that she was organized when it came to the trinkets. She had them arrayed on the shelves in alphabetical order. Once I realized that I skipped over to the L's to search for lamps.

Many shapes and sizes adorned the shelf. I decided to give the camera another try and brought it up to look through the lens. Three of them sparkled but only one was tiny.

I reached out to grab the trinket.

"Stop," Seth said in a stern voice. Not the voice you'd imagine a seven-year old would possess. I halted my grab for the item.

"Why?"

He cocked his head to one side with narrowed eyes. "Do you think my grandmother would not have placed some sort of protection on her precious items?"

Oops. The kid was right. Now that I focused on the area I felt an electrical current that buzzed under my hand as if warning me to try and take the item from the shelf. I pulled my hand back and turned around. "Thanks, that would have been a huge blunder."

"Again," Seth said and tapped his head. "You're not too bright, are you?"

"Ugh. I was excited, okay? Everyone makes mistakes."

"Yes, but if I wasn't here then you would have been a messy mistake splatter all over Granny's office and yours truly would have had to clean it up."

Why make a young boy clean up the mess? Doesn't Mrs. Smith have a cleaning staff on hand to take care of such things? A thought occurred to me from what I heard of their conversation last night. "She's not really your grandmother, is she?"

"Why would you ask that?" He frowned. "Of course she's my grandmother."

I wasn't buying it not after I heard him call her 'master.'

"Because I heard you call her 'master' last night when I left the dining room."

He was quiet for a while before he answered, "Look. We don't have all day to discuss whether I am or am not related to my grandmother. And I know you're on a tight schedule."

I kept my mouth shut. He was right that I didn't have the luxury to chit chat all day. Glenda needed the artifact or I might as well head on back to Avarice to become her next zombie minion.

Seth continued, "I know my Granny would probably want to trade you the trinket for that camera. It's the only way you'll get what you want unless you happen to know how to disarm a protection spell."

"Does Mary know how to undo the spell?" I asked.

He shook his head. "She did not know last night but I guarantee that she'll be back with the know-how later. So do you want the artifact or not?"

Doors opened and slammed in the hallway. The footsteps got closer when Mrs. Smith called out, "Seth? Are you in here?"

CHAPTER
TWENTY-ONE

LIGHTS FLARED to life when Mrs. Smith's hand flipped the switch to her office. She stood there with Mary standing behind her and Gray not too far away. Her cold determined eyes swept the room and landed on me.

"What are you doing in my office?" Mrs. Smith said with a slight shrill in her voice.

I winced and pocketed my hands from where they hovered over the shelves near the lamps.

"I was looking for Seth," I lied and motioned towards where he sat in the overstuffed leather chair behind the desk. His feet were no longer propped up but were firmly set on the floor while he glowered at his grandmother.

The two exchanged glances and moved their eyes like they were speaking mentally to one another. I kept hoping that she wouldn't round back on me with more questions.

"Grandson," Mrs. Smith said. "Why are you in my office?"

"I was looking for something to read, grandmother."

"And why is she here?" Mrs. Smith gestured to me. Welp, guess staying still didn't matter with this woman.

I stepped forward away from the shelf with my hands in my pockets and replied, "Like I said, I was looking for your grandson, Seth."

The elderly woman's shrewd eyes narrowed a fraction more and she replied, "No, you were not."

Mary's own eyes were wide and she held her breath like she knew something big was about to happen and it was not going to be good. Gray kept a neutral expression on his face and observed from his spot out in the hallway.

I took another step and leaned my butt against the desk and crossed my arms. "Okay, what was I doing, Mrs. Smith?"

A brash snarl escaped the old woman's lips when she spoke. "You were trying to steal from me."

My butt slipped half an inch and I fell off to the side taking with me the piles of papers on top of the desk. Several leafs of paper sliced through the air on their descent to the ground and tried to find purchase in my exposed skin. Death by a thousand paper cuts if I was lucky enough but I knew that the storm had only started.

Mrs. Smith stomped on the worn carpet to where I landed on the floor under all the paperwork that had fallen on top. Her eyes glowed a molten gold as she sneered down at me. Her face taking on more draconic attributes. "I don't take kindly to thieves."

"Um," I said and licked my lips. Well, if I'm going down then

I'm not going alone. I darted my eyes over to Mary, pointed and blurted out, "I'm not alone. Mary's in on it too."

"Oh, bitch, I know you didn't," Mary said.

Our elderly host whirled around and was on Mary in an instant. She poked her bony fingers into Mary's chest and asked, "Are you not with her?"

Seth chimed in. "I can confirm they're in cahoots with each other, grandmother."

"What?" Both Mary and I said in unison.

Mrs. Smith straightened up and brushed her outfit off before she turned to Gray who stood idle in the hallway.

"Gray, show these ruffians out. I will not give them any more opportunities to steal from my precious collection."

"Of course, madam." He nodded his head and waited for her to leave.

On her way down the hall she yelled, "Seth, with me, now."

Seth scrambled out of his chair, hopped over the desk and out the door before I had a chance to blink. Gray swept the mountain of papers off of me and helped me up. He dusted my outfit off with swats that were heavier than they needed to be to brush dust off of clothes.

Mary tried to edge her way down the hall when Gray's steely eyes pinned her against the wall. "Stay there Ms. Dawn. I'd hate to use other means to make you listen and follow directions."

She halted and watched as Gray took both my wrists, clamped them behind my back and steered me out of the room. He pushed me against the wall and closed the door right behind him. The doors locked when they closed with an audible click of the latch.

"This way, ladies." He grabbed a hold of my wrists and pushed me down the hallway. Mary trailed behind but not too far since Gray appeared to be in no mood for any shenanigans from either of us.

When we entered the foyer of the house our luggage was waiting for us to pick up before we left the house. Gray let go of my hands and straightened his jacket. I rubbed my wrists which were sore from his strong grip. Strength that a man of his age should not possess. The more I stayed at this house the more I realized there was more beneath the surface. Nothing was as it seemed.

Gray walked to the front door and opened it while gesturing towards the exit. "Ladies, I believe your welcome has run out. Please leave or else."

The way he said 'or else' sent chills down my spine. Like if we didn't leave then he would be free to exercise whatever persuasion of his choosing to make us leave or wish we had left when we had the chance.

Mary grabbed her bags, walked over to me and said, "This ain't over."

She stomped down the stairs and hustled over to Betsy and threw her bags in the back. She unlocked the truck, hopped in and started her up with no backfires. I stood there watching and then it dawned on me. My sleep deprived brain finally registered that Mary was stealing my ride.

I snatched my bags up from the ground, ran out the door waving my arms and yelled, "Hey."

Betsy was already on the move by the time I made it to the

round driveway from the door and down the many steps. Mary shifted her into higher gear and sped down the path.

Knowing that there was no chance that I could have caught up I slowed down to a stop and dropped my bag. I watched Betsy's tailgate fade off into the distance with Mary's middle finger held prominently in the rear window as she waved it back and forth in a farewell salute. I grounded my teeth, kicked my bag and shouted after Mary, "You bitch."

Her laughter echoed back to where I stood and I kicked my bag again. "Damnit."

The clock was ticking and I had only two hours left before Glenda expected me to bring her the trinket. I glanced back at the mansion, then back down the driveway and let out another huff. The migraine from yesterday was threatening to come back again. If I could have all the time in the world like Mary then that would be ideal but that wasn't happening. I only had one option at this point and I didn't like it.

TO BE FAIR, Mrs. Smith was reasonable once I was able to give her my version of the story. She even called Glenda on my behalf to persuade her to give me more time. Of course, in exchange I had to help her catch Mary. Which is how yours truly ended up back in the dusty old office sitting in the worn-down rickety leather chair.

The chair's cushioning where it counted was non-existent. I didn't see how Seth could have been comfortable in it earlier today. My eyes burned because I was still running on fumes. I didn't have the luxury for a nap because Mrs. Smith and Seth were adamant that Mary would be back and they were unsure when she would make her attempt to steal said trinket that I was after earlier.

Dust tickled the inside of my nose and I tried my best to not sneeze. No use. The dust was persistent and continued to assault my sinuses until I let loose a loud sneeze. But not one, but several of them in succession. By the time I was finished there was spit and snot on top of the desk and running down my face. Yes, I know, glamorous. The latest fade, let me tell you, all the gals were wearing facial snot to their galas this year. Ew, no. Just no.

I looked around for some paper to transfer the gross slime that adorned my face so that I could feel somewhat clean once more. Didn't help that it triggered another round of sneeze-fest. I was not a fan. Would not recommend a sneeze-fest.

As I blew my nose offerings into a poor unsuspecting piece of paper, I heard a low chuckle. I glanced around the darkened room and asked, "Who's there?"

No answer.

Though, I swore I saw something move in the dark corner of the room. I shook my head and let my eyes readjust. They were watery from all the sneezing. The longer the night went on the more I was jumping at shadows. Not to mention I needed to pee again. The sneezing did not help my case. I sat in the chair crossing and uncrossing my legs to help alleviate the pressure.

Then when everything got quiet I heard the small 'tink' like glass was knocked over and landed on the floor. I stayed put in the chair so as not to alarm our intruder. The window over on the right became unlatched by a dark gloved hand and slid up slowly with care.

After the window was opened the figure in a sleek black ninja suit stepped into the room with no sound. They tiptoed around the haphazard piles of paper and went directly to the shelf with the lamps. Angelic words were spoken followed by a flash of blue. The hum in the room, which apparently was there in the background and I had assumed was air conditioning, came to a stop.

The person moved the lamps aside searching for a specific one. While they were in the process of looking, I sniffled, the person suddenly straightened up and whirled around. Ninja stars bit into the back of the leather chair where I sat. I held up one of my hands while the other kept a good firm grip on my camera, "Whoa. Easy there tiger."

They came closer, with narrowed amber eyes and gestured at the camera.

"You should not have that," the person hissed in a low gravelly voice. "Give it to me."

I rolled my eyes. "Cut the crap, Mary. I know it's you."

The ninja halted their footsteps, waited a moment, let out a huff and yanked the bottom portion of their mask down. She replied, "What gave me away?"

"Your interest in this camera and that you came back for the lamp."

"Lamp?" She arched an eyebrow. "I don't know what you're talking about."

"Ha, bullshit." I laughed and gestured at the lamps. "You were looking in the collection of lamps, just now."

She glowered for a moment before her eyes widened like something dawned on her. She hopped away from me, pointed while she backed up to the window and said, "Oh hell no. A trap? Blondie, you set me up?"

"Guilty as charged." I smiled and raised my camera.

Mary swallowed hard and waved her hands back and forth.

"Please, don't. You have no idea what you're about to do with that camera."

"Oh really?" I furrowed my brow. "I think I do."

She got closer to the window and said, "No, bitch, you don't."

Mary pointed for me to put the camera down. She pulled out an item and it glowed a bright azure blue. It burned my eyes from the sudden brightness in the room.

Tears welled up in my eyes, but I held onto the camera with it aimed straight at Mary and said, "Mrs. Smith was kind enough to tell me what this camera did and why it ate its previous hosts within seven days. She also told me how to prevent it from happening. Do you know what that is?"

Mary held the object in her hand in front like a person holding a crucifix up to a vampire. Her teeth clenched while she continued to back away. "Of course I know. Why they fuck do you think I was trying to get that camera away from you?"

"I need to hear it," I chirped and ignored the searing pain I felt on my arm. "Say it."

"You feed it other life forces to save your own."

The window behind her slammed shut. She jumped.

"See? Was that so hard?" I said. "Now be a good girl and say cheese."

TWENTY-THREE

SLOW GOLF CLAPS happened from the darkened corner of the room. Mary and I both turned our heads towards the sound. Seth stepped out of the shadows, his eyes shone like fire.

"Bravo, bra-vo," he said as he continued to clap. Around his neck hung the small lamp that I found in the office earlier. The blue azure light lit his features and I swore that it wavered between the young boy to the man in his late twenties with well-toned muscles.

Mary whirled the lit item his way and shouted, "Stay back."

He chuckled and toyed with the small trinket on his neck. Seth looked over at me and said, "I didn't think you'd have it in you, Sarah. To take another's life to save your own. I guess Granny wins this bet."

"I'm still here," Mary said.

"Of course." Seth nodded. "I was sent to make sure you lived."

"Well, I'm just gonna hop on out of here then—" Mary said, placing the glowing object in her mouth and trying to slide open the window. It did not budge. "C'mon open."

My finger itched to depress the button. I took my hand away and shook it to get rid of the tingles. Seth glanced at me before he stepped closer to Mary.

"Look." He placed a hand on her and she paused. Her eyes were wet but she refused to let any tears fall. Seth reached for the artifact that he had on his person and held it up to Mary.

I got up and moved towards them but Seth shook his head. His eyes darted my way before he looked back at Mary. He said, "I know both of you were looking for this lamp."

"It's my lamp," he admitted. "So, it's my choice on who will earn it tonight."

The azure light dimmed and Mary took it from her mouth and held it in her hand. Her lips pressed together into a firm line as she looked between me, Seth and the window.

"That's it?" Mary asked. The usual fire in her voice was coming back. "What about Mrs. Smith? I thought she owned the trinket."

Seth shook his head. "No. She thinks she does but, no."

Wait, what? If he's a genie of a lamp then how would Mrs. Smith not own him? Aren't those who possess the lamp the genie's masters? Him calling the old woman 'master' the other night now made perfect sense. However, now he said she wasn't his master? How?

"I see you have several questions running through your mind, Sarah," Seth said. "Answer my questions correctly and you'll learn the truth. Answer them wrong, and well..." He shrugged his shoulders and held the other hand up and wobbled it.

Mary tried the window again. "Open this window, demon."

Okay, now I was really confused. Obviously, Seth was a genie, not a demon. I was about to correct her when Seth interjected. "She's right Sarah. I am a demon. A special kind of demon."

"Fine," Mary spat. "I'll play your game. If I win, then I get the camera, the lamp and my life."

"Agreed." Seth bobbed his head.

Mary added, "And I get to leave unharmed, and no one follows me. Got it?"

"Of course," Seth said and turned back to me. "Sarah, how about you? Are you in agreement?"

"Everything except my camera. It's mine." I hugged the camera close to my body and pulled it away from the group.

"That's not what you agreed with earlier, Sarah." Seth's eyes narrowed. "You had a deal with Mrs. Smith, remember?"

"Fine," I grumbled and turned back around. "I'm all in."

Seth clapped then rubbed his hands together and wore an impish smile when he asked, "Now, how good are you at guessing the Sphinx's riddles?"

"Hold up." I held my hand up and continued, "My deal with Mrs. Smith was to deliver the thief to her in exchange for the trinket."

Seth raised his eyebrow. "Do you really believe that old dragon, Mrs. Smith, would allow you to leave these premises with any of her treasures? Especially with that camera? After you promised it to her?"

My cheeks flushed but I slapped my hand on the desk, dust wafting up from the surface, and argued, "That was the deal."

He looked over at Mary. "I see what you mean. She really isn't all that bright."

"Nope." Mary smiled. "It's a miracle that she's lasted this long."

"Hey," I protested and slapped the desk again. More dust flew into the airthreatening my sinuses and I grabbed for more paper.

Mary rolled her hand and said, "You mentioned riddles?"

"Ah, yes," Seth replied. "Let us continue our little competition. The one who wins can leave unharmed, unfollowed and with my lamp. As for the camera, um, well, we'll discuss that when we get to it."

He walked away from the desk and back to the bookcase to lean up against it. His gold eyes glowing in the dark shadows of the room. Seth said, "First one who earns three points wins. Are you ready?"

Mary replied, "Yes."

"Just get on with it," I said and huffed.

"Fine, since you're getting all moody then Mary can go first." Seth frowned then looked over at her and asked, "Amongst two sisters, the first one gives birth to the other and she further gives birth to the first. Who are they?"

"Oh, that one is easy," she cooed. "Especially since I read Oedipus."

"Not fair," I cried. "Her answer shouldn't count since she's read the story and knows the answer."

Seth glowered. "Sarah, sit down and stop interrupting. Mary, what is your answer?"

Mary tapped her chin and acted like she needed to think of her answer. She replied, "The sisters are, Day and Night."

"Correct." Seth turned to me. "Okay miss whiney pants it's your turn now. I'll make sure this one is easy because you feel Mary had an unfair advantage. It's not my fault that she reads. You might benefit from that activity from time to time."

"Stereotype much?" I spat back at him.

He let out a low chuckle then asked, "What has hands and a face, but can't hold anything or a smile?"

Mary's eyes went wide, and she waved her hand for Seth to call on her. I smacked the desk again and said, "Mary this is my riddle. Not yours."

"What is your answer, Sarah?" Seth asked.

"Give me a minute."

What has hands and a face, but can't hold anything or even smile? Hmm. Hands and face but can't smile. The others in the room waited for me to reply. I should know the answer to this and the riddle was supposed to be simple. What would have hands and a face but not be able to smile?

"Seth, you should call time. Sarah doesn't know the answer."

"No, no," Seth replied. "Give her a chance. It'll come to her, we have all the time we need."

They may have had all the time in the world but the clock was ticking away for me. I smacked my forehead. The answer was obvious. A clock had arms and a face but definitely could not hold anything or even smile.

I replied, "A clock."

"Took you long enough," Mary quipped under her breath.

Ugh. I grabbed the camera and held it up, "Don't make me use this."

"Ladies, ladies." Seth motioned with his hands for us to settle down. "We're at one to one. Let's keep going, shall we?"

We both nodded for Seth to continue. He said, "The first to answer gets the next point… I disappear in the dark and appear in the day. You cannot feel me if you touch me."

"Shadow," Mary said while the words were barely formed on my lips.

"Point to Mary." Seth nodded. "That's two to one."

I leaned forward and strained my ears to listen to the next riddle. If Mary won then she would get the lamp and maybe my camera. And yours truly would end up in servitude to Mrs. Smith for all eternity or depending on her mood as her next BBQ dinner. I shuddered.

Seth looked between us and asked, "I never was, am always to be. No one ever saw me, nor ever will, and yet I am the confidence of all who live and breathe. What am I?"

I knew this one. For once in my life I actually knew this riddle. It was a favorite riddle used by many members of *SUM*.

"Tomorrow," we both shouted.

Seth inclined his head my way. "Point to Sarah."

"Bullshit," Mary argued. "We both said it. I should get the point too."

"Sarah was a fraction faster," he replied. "If you both continue to throw fits then I will start to take away points. Is that what you want to happen?"

"No," we both said in a solemn tone.

"Good."

Mary and I were tied once more. Two to two. There was no way that I was a fraction faster. We both said the answer at the same time. But heck if I was going to correct Seth. I needed to win this contest or kiss everything goodbye. I had no desire to be a zombie slave, a dragon minion or a BBQ special - extra crispy.

"Last one. So, listen carefully." Seth held his hands in his pocket. The scene struck me as something familiar as he rocked back and forth on his feet like he was fidgeting with an object.

"What do I have in my pocket?" He grinned.

"Oh hell, no, you didn't," Mary said and moved her head in a sass bob. She pointed at him. "You're trying to trick us. I ain't gonna answer that phony riddle."

After watching *The Hobbit* a bazillion times and the scene with Bilbo Baggins and Golum. I knew the exact answer and replied, "The ring that rules them all."

Seth beamed at me as he pulled out a golden ring. "Not exactly but close enough."

Mary smacked her forehead. "You've got to be kidding me. That wasn't a riddle."

"Yes," Seth replied in a scholarly fashion. "It was. Not my fault you didn't bother to answer."

"But you cheated," Mary whined and rubbed her temples. "I was a fool to fall for this. Blondie must be rubbing off on me because I would never have agreed to this competition."

I stuck my tongue out at Mary and said, "I won fair and square. You're just a sore loser."

Seth placed the lamp down on the desk in front of me and

replied, "You won. As agreed you get the lamp, your life and the camera. Now, leave."

"Aren't you coming? I mean, aren't you tied to the lamp?"

"Yes, in a way, I am, but I can go a long way from the lamp. I will come… soon. Need to address some final details to rework agreements with the dragon. Mary, please come with me."

"Nuh-uh." Her head whipped back up and she threw the heaviest books at the window. Glass shattered outwards while Mary lunged towards the desk. She grabbed the lamp and my camera before she stepped back.

My hands scrabbled to hold onto the strap but Mary yanked it free and dove out the window. I scrambled to my feet and rushed to the broken window in time to see Mary crash in the hedges below and tumble to the ground.

Her feet landed and she darted to her ride hidden within the shadows. Her motorcycle rumbled to life and she streaked down the driveway with both artifacts in her hands. Why didn't I hear her come up on that monstrosity? Oh, right. I live in a world of magic and she probably used a silencing spell on it to mask her arrival.

I stood there with my mouth hung open and at a loss for words.

For once, I had won fair and square only to be swindled from both of my prizes. Deep within the mansion I heard the loud roars of a beast who was well aware of treasures lost. I swallowed the hard lump in my throat and turned my head to Seth.

He was looking down the hallway when he waved his hand at me to leave. "You better go. Now would be good. I'll handle her."

I went to him, looked over his shoulder down the hall and asked, "How can you still be here when Mary took your lamp?"

"It's complicated." He frowned. "Here."

Seth pressed into my hands something small and round. It was the ring from earlier. "Use this when you absolutely need to. It will only work once. Don't waste it."

"And Mrs. Smith?" I asked while I backed away to the window. Thunderous steps boomed in the household. "What about her? And my deal with her?"

"I'll take care of it," Seth replied. "Now go. Glenda is waiting."

I knocked more of the glass shards out of the window and positioned myself ready to jump down into the hedges. If Mary could do it then so could I. It was only a story drop… not too far from the ground.

"Go, now," Seth yelled.

Behind me I heard the earth shattering roar of a dragon. The hairs on my body stood on end when the workings of magic became thick within the room. Heat flared and pushed me out the window into the bushes below. I landed hard and stumbled away from the clinging twigs and branches.

More fire erupted from the office above and I flinched. This was no time to gawk and wait for Mrs. Smith to catch me. I started running as fast as my legs could run. My borrowed time was out, I still needed to meet with Glenda, empty handed and she was going to rip out my throat.

TWENTY-FOUR

THE ROARS from the mansion still echoed down the road I ran on. My ribs caught on each breath that I sucked in between gasps for air. I wasn't physically fit, never needed to be athletic nor did anyone from *SUM* even bother to tell me that I should probably take up running.

Nope. I would have stopped a block ago if I didn't hear the roars but I got startled and ran more to get away from the dragon that wanted to roast my bones for betraying her. I couldn't help that tonight's dealings went south and she never got her new minion. Nor could I help that Seth did his own double dealings.

None of this made sense. If he was a genie, then how was he not required to follow his lamp? What was his original deal with Mrs. Smith? And why the hell did I feel cold all over? I had been running for a while and I was cold?

My teeth chattered while I ran, and I rubbed my arms to ward off the chills that I felt all over. I slowed down, walking at a snail's pace and blew into my cold hands. The night was a balmy eighty degrees and here I was freezing.

The ground shifted in front of me and I stopped. Walter's form rose up from the dirt and he stood with his arms crossed. His lips were pressed into a thin line that curved downward.

"I told you this would not end well," he chided me.

"Sh-hh-u-t up," I stuttered between teeth chattering and chills that wracked my body.

"You should not have listened to my mother. Now look at you. Lost not one but two artifacts, have an angry dragon after you—"

"D-d-don't forget the sex demon." I tried to smile.

Walter placed his hand on my shoulder. It did not feel cold which alarmed me that something wasn't right.

"Walter," I said through shivers. "Why aren't you cold?"

"Your life force is being depleted."

Panic shot through me. The camera.

Walter continued, "The longer you are apart from that cursed camera, the more it will take. You have to get it back before it steals your life."

I rested my head against his chest, not paying attention to the smell of death, and groaned. "I have no way of finding that woman or even have any means of transportation."

He patted and rubbed my back. Gave me a brief hug before he pushed me away.

"I'm sorry. And I'm sorry to say that my reasons for being here are not in your favor either. Avarice has told me that she wants to meet tonight. She knows you have the camera and wants to discuss your double dealings."

"Why would she want to discuss that? The snake tattoo would have killed me if I wasn't acting in accordance with her rules."

He tapped my tattoo. "That's part of why she wants to talk."

"Huh?" My brow furrowed.

"Look. Meet her at this address." Walter handed me a folded up piece of paper. On it was the written address where I was to meet with Avarice.

"And if I don't come?"

He stared down at me. His fingers tapped on his crossed arms. "You know what happens if you do not show."

Right. Death by zombie horde. It is by far the most gruesome death and one that I did not want to experience myself. I nodded. "I will be there. I promise."

"Be sure that you do," Walter said and sunk down into the ground and was swallowed up by the earth.

I texted Glenda and grimaced. "Come get me. Got artifact."

TWENTY-FIVE

GLENDA'S expensive sedan pulled up next to me where I waited. My only guess as to how she found me was magic. In a world full of magic the impossible became probably and most likely to happen. That or it was her werewolf heritage that allowed her to pick up my scent not too far from Mrs. Smith's house. I'm going with option two.

She rolled down the window and lowered her shades. A half-werewolf wearing shades at night? One glance at her yellow eyes told me her powers were almost at full capacity with the full moon happening tomorrow night. Or was it tonight?

Glenda held out her hand and said, "Give it to me."

"What?" I asked. "No 'hey, how are you? Are you okay?'"

"Quit stalling and give me the lamp," she growled.

"Um." I continued to rub my arms and looked around my surroundings. Nothing seemed to help the dense cold that sunk deep within my bones.

Her other hand clenched the steering wheel, the leather creaked and the shape warped under sheer pressure. Glenda snarled. "You said you had the artifact. Was that a lie?"

"I had *an* artifact. Not *the* artifact."

My hand reached into my pocket and pulled out the golden ring that Seth gave me earlier. I showed it to her as it glinted in the moonlight.

"That's a toy, you moron. I did not send you to go get a replica of the ring from *Lord of the Rings*."

Was it a replica? I squinted at it in the street lamp and moonlight. The ring had the elvish language scrawled on the inside and outside of the ring. Son-of-a-biscuit. Seth tricked me.

"Give me one good reason why I should not rip your throat out here and now?"

My stomach plummeted. "Um."

A voice smooth as silk spoke as a masculine hand was placed on Glenda's hand on the steering wheel. He said, "Let me handle this."

Glenda let out a sigh and the yellow in her eyes faded upon skin contact with the man in the vehicle. Uh-oh. Not him again. Hearing his voice sent butterflies through me and started up my core deep down. I thought I lost him but he was here and was using Glenda to get to me.

"Sarah." Vincent's velvety voice crooned from within the sedan. "Do you know where the artifact is?"

I must resist his charm. He was laying it on thick and you could practically feel the sexual emotions rolling off of him and out of the car. The cold sensation that I felt was warm with the buzz of sexual tension. I stood there in a daze.

The sound of a door opening and closing did not register until I felt his large smooth hands grab ahold of my upper arms and he leaned in to whisper, "Yes, I know you like this. Your body is practically melting into my embrace. I can give you more but I need something from you first."

Leaning more into his chest, seeking out the warmth, I snuggled deep and let out a moan. He moved his hands down to wrap me into his arms. He rubbed the length of my chilled arms, trying to warm me up. I was literally putty in his hands.

Vincent leaned in, letting his lips brush against my ear and breathed, "Where is the artifact?"

Tingles shot through me and I couldn't resist. I whispered in a dreamy voice, "Mary. She has them."

"Them?" he purred. "Wasn't it one artifact?"

"No, two," I replied and hung in his arms like a limp noodle. "The camera is an artifact too."

Glenda interrupted us. "You lost them, both? You idiot."

The sexual buzz that I felt dissipated, and I realized who was holding me up. I leapt away from him and did a jig to ward off his sex cooties. With both my index fingers crossed over each other and held up to him I said, "Stay away from me."

Vincent only arched one of his slender, well manicured eyebrows up at me. The corner of his mouth lifted into a slight smirk. He turned to Glenda, "What do you want to do, boss?"

Boss? What? Since when? I was about to ask when Glenda rolled her eyes and snapped back at him. "Obviously, you will go retrieve those artifacts for me. I would do it myself but I have other tasks to attend to tonight."

"Of course." He bowed. "Though consider that after tonight

my debt to you, paid in full."

"Fine." She scowled. "And take that idiot with you. Maybe she'll learn how to do something right for a change. I have no idea what my dear Walter saw in her."

"Mmm." Vincent walked behind me like a wolf prowling around his prey. He leaned into my hair and inhaled. "This one owes me. Let me take her off of your hands after we retrieve the artifacts for you. Then I'll owe you another favor."

The half-werewolf drummed her fingers on the steering wheel in contemplation of Vincent's offer. If Vincent got his way then I was screwed, until either the camera stole the rest of my life-force, the dragon found me to char my flesh, zombie hordes descended on my mutinous hide, or Avarice had a change of heart and decided to add me to her zombie collection. So much goodness to look forward to and in so little time.

"No," Glenda replied. "She's mine. Whatever she owes you, I will pay."

"Are you sure?" he purred and slid his hand onto my shoulder. I shrugged him off.

"Quite." Glenda showed her sharp elongated teeth in challenge. "She's mine."

Vincent nodded, held up his hands and stepped away from me. "Of course."

She glanced down at her expensive watch and began to roll up her window. I held out my hand and shouted, "Wait. Aren't you going to drive us?"

"No, you idiot. I still have no idea what Walter sees in you," she replied and shook her head. The car drove off as she called out, "Call an Uber."

WE DID CALL AN UBER. Vincent had the more technological advance phone that allowed him to hail an Uber from our location. We still had no idea where Mary took off to but Vincent wanted to pick up the trail back at Mrs. Smith's place.

I highly objected to going back to the dragon but I had no say in where we went since Vincent paid for our ride. The driver showed up in a nondescript gray sedan. The paint had seen better years, but the car ran smooth. He drove us to Mrs. Smith's place and waited outside the iron entry gates per Vincent's instructions.

"Hey, can you crank up the heat in here?" I asked the driver. "I'm freezing."

"Lady," the driver replied. "It's like eighty degrees and ninety percent humid outside. I'm not going to turn on the heat. You crazy or something?"

I flopped back down in my seat with a big over dramatic sigh and rubbed my arms. My teeth continued to chatter while chills caused me to shiver. Vincent gave me a wry look before he unbuckled his seat belt.

The sex demon hopped out of the car and went to the gates. His nose in the air trying to catch a scent. He whirled around and crooked his finger at me to get out of the car. Hell, if I wanted to even be this close to the dragon that wanted to roast my bones for dinner. I merely escaped her wrath not an hour ago and now the sex demon wanted to try our luck? For what?

I mouthed, "No." And shook my head.

Vincent frowned and placed his hands on his hips. He glanced back towards Mrs. Smith's house and back at the car. Chewed his bottom lip for a moment then nodded before he walked back to the car. The demon opened my door.

"Hey," I protested.

"Do you have something of hers?" Vincent asked.

"What?"

"This Mary person. Do you have something of hers?"

"Besides a bruised ego?"

"Not helping, Sarah."

"No. I don't."

He rubbed his chin. "Mmm. This will make it much more difficult to track her. But let me try."

The demon leaned in, his nose close to my skin and I shoved him away. "Excuse you."

He blinked his eyes and grimaced. "I am trying to grab a scent. She was close to you tonight, yes? Then I will pick it out from yours."

Ick. Don't get me wrong, Vincent is a handsome fellow and if he didn't use his powers for wrong or to overpower women to get sex then I might have felt something genuine towards him. But as of right now, each encounter that I'd had with him he'd used my libido against me to get what he wanted.

Vincent leaned in once more and inhaled deep. His nose brushed over me along with the stubble from his five o'clock shadow prickling my skin. Gooseflesh erupted from where he touched me with a whisper. I told the butterflies in my stomach to give it a rest. I didn't have time to be sexually flustered on top of freezing to death.

His eyes opened when he caught a scent that he could use. He walked a few steps from the car and circled around sniffing the air. Vincent paused, closed his eyes and took one more sniff before he snapped his fingers and spoke words that were not for human lips.

A red line faded into view and streamed down the road. The line went around a corner and continued onward. Satisfied, Vincent bent down, patted my leg and closed the door. He hopped back into the car on the other side and buckled up.

The driver sat in his seat with his mouth hung open. He rubbed his eyes several times and mumbled, "I must be dreaming. This can't be real."

"Welcome to the crazy world of magic," I said under my breath.

Vincent patted the back of the drivers chair and gestured at the red guide. "Follow that line."

CHAPTER
TWENTY-SEVEN

OUR GUIDE, the red line that hung in the air, led us back to the motel that I had stayed at when I first came into town. I had no idea. What were the chances they'd be at the same motel? Betsy sat outside the room in all her rust bucket glory. Along with the sleek crotch rocket motorcycle that Mary escaped on earlier tonight.

The sight of Betsy made my heart fill with hope, maybe Ivan was here? Perhaps he could help talk sense into Mary and make her give me the artifacts? Of course, he might not, considering I stole his truck and left him high and dry at the gas station. But I'm going to pray that maybe he would be willing to help me out because everyone deserves a second chance.

Lights were still on in the room when Vincent and I exited the car and crept up to the room's window to listen in on the conversation. Inside I could hear Ivan and Mary arguing over the artifacts. Good, Ivan was here. I held my breath and listened, hoping for the right moment to knock on their door.

"Mary, you took this artifact?" Ivan asked with a sharp pang in his voice. "We only needed the lamp. You should not have taken this one too."

"Blondie almost used it on me, Ivan. On me," Mary replied. "She doesn't have a single good bone in her body. That's why I took it. To keep people like her from using the artifact."

"But it will kill her," he argued. "Are you okay with that?"

"Hey, it's one less bad person."

"No." He smacked his hand on a hard surface. "We don't say who lives and dies. It's not our way. We should help her. Not leave her to die."

"Ivan, did you forget she stole your truck?" Mary said then added, "Twice."

His voice rumbled in a deep chuckle and let it roll into laughter. "No, no, I did not. But I will not hold that against her."

"I do."

Ivan clucked his tongue. "No, no, no. Do not hold on to that hate. Release and forgive. For it is who we are, yah?"

"Ugh. As much as I hate to admit you're right."

"Good. Now, we must go find and help her."

Mary's voice became bright when she said, "Last I saw her she was about to be charred bbq by the dragon."

"You left her?" Ivan shouted and the sound of a chair scraped across the floor. "Mary, you know better."

"Hey," Mary argued. "She had the help of the djinn so I think she made it out okay. He appeared to have taken a liking to her.

Besides, she was already in heaps of trouble way before the dragon decided to flame the office."

"Mary." Ivan slapped the hard surface again. "You will come with me to go save her. No buts. We will go now."

"No."

A struggle sounded and chairs clattered to the ground. Vincent and I couldn't see much past the curtains. But we did see shadows. Ivan appeared to have held Mary's arm and she looked down at his hand. She said, "If you want to keep that hand of yours then I suggest you let me go, now."

"You are being difficult. Is there nothing I can do to make you come with me?"

"No. You're on your own if you want to go save Blondie."

"Fine. I will go. You stay here. Our contact will be here soon to take the artifacts for containment."

"Okay, go then. I've got this."

Ivan let go of Mary's arm and readjusted his jacket. He walked over and picked up the chair that was knocked over during their scuffle. A hand grabbed the back of my collar and dragged me back to the shadows between the buildings.

The door to Mary and Ivan's room opened and Ivan walked out. He strolled over to Betsy and caressed her hood with his left hand. His eyes searched around and hovered on each dark shadow seeking for any potential danger. Vincent held his hand over my mouth to stifle the cold air that escaped my lips while we watched Ivan get into the truck.

Betsy sputtered to life with the familiar backfire that greeted the driver. Vincent pulled me further back into the shadows and we ducked behind the dumpster to hide from Ivan when he turned Betsy's lights on. The truck puttered out of the parking lot and went in the direction of Mrs. Smith's house to be my knight in shining armor. Too bad I wasn't there.

We both heard the door shut to the room and Vincent motioned for me to follow him. He paused and whispered, "Let me go in first. I'll handle the spitfire, you grab the artifacts, deal?"

I nodded and followed his lead.

Vincent straightened up when he got to the door. His hand poised to knock when I stepped in front of him.

"You can't just knock on the door. You crazy?" I whispered as loud as I could without it becoming not a whisper.

"Sarah, I know what I'm doing. Now move. Go hide for now until I call you over." He tried to shoo me away but I refused to budge.

"Do you really want me to use my powers on you?" He leaned in close with his lips a fraction from mine. The butterflies swirled around in my core and reminded me of the delicious feeling that he gave me when he did use his powers.

I shook my head. "C'mon. She'll see right through you. She's not dumb."

"Oh, so she's not like you?" he replied with a smirk.

"Ass." I tried to shove him away but he crushed me up against the door and kissed me long and deep that had my core pumping away. He pulled back and blew out a breath that formed a mist. His smirk still in place, while he stroked my cheek.

And then the door opened. Vincent and I fell backwards and landed on the floor with a loud thump. My mind was still reeling from the kiss when Mary stood over us and said, "Oh, hell, no."

VINCENT SHOT UP and slammed into Mary before she could react. He pushed her up against the fall wall, his hand over her mouth and arm pressed firm on her chest to secure her in place. Below his right leg pinned her legs to prevent her from escaping.

I was still on the ground and watched with round eyes at the speed of his movements. Yes, I knew he was a demon. A sex demon. But never had I ever seen him display those abilities. The ones that I knew of were suggestions from a mere touch, sexual impulses and charm.

He hissed over his shoulder. "Sarah, quit gawking and get the artifacts."

"Right," I said and pushed myself back up. "On it."

"Argh," Vincent cried and flicked his hand up and down. "She licked me."

"Release my legs and I'll do a lot more than that," Mary said with more venom than was needed in her voice. "And Blondie, don't you dare touch those artifacts."

I was homing in on the camera and the lamp that sat on the table. My hand was in mid-reach when Mary told me to stop. An electric undercurrent could be felt just above them like the table had a forcefield in place.

"Vinny, we've got a problem," I called out. "There's a forcefield."

"Then disable it," he replied while he struggled with Mary against the wall. She lunged for his ear and tried to take a bite out of his lobe. He barely moved his head to the side to miss her attack.

"I don't know how." My teeth worried my bottom lip.

"You serious?" Vincent replied. "How in the seven hells do you not know how to disable that? It's the easiest one in the book. My lord you're an idiot."

Mary laughed. "And you're just now catching on that she ain't too bright? Maybe you should join her club."

"Shut up." He pressed his arm up against her neck. Her body lifted from the ground and she scrambled with her hands to stop Vincent from strangling her. He eased up and let her toes gain some purchase. With a stern look he said, "Don't move."

I searched the table to see if I could disable it. It's not like they never trained me. Come on, come on, think. I closed my eyes. Think back to your training with Walter. I knew he covered this with me once upon a time. The memory was hazy but I listened to the conversation.

"Now Sarah." Walter slid his arms around and pulled me in close to him. "This one is easy. Just close your eyes and feel the power."

I closed my eyes and held out my hands feeling the vibrations hum through my palm and fingertips.

Walter's lips brushed close to my ear and whispered, "Follow the current. Feel where it is the strongest. Where it pools. Yes, that's it."

My hands followed the tingles until they felt like several pins and needles were sliding in and out of my hands and arms. I held it above the area where it was the strongest.

Below my right hand the current was the strongest and I snapped my eyes open. The power source was another object that glowed a bright azure blue. How did I miss this?

"I found the power source," I said aloud and turned. Vincent had Mary unconscious and was busy zip tying her hands behind her back and her feet. He stood up and dusted his hands off.

"Good." He walked over and glanced at the object. With a wave of his hand he said words that sounded like hissing before the blue azure object faded off.

I blinked and asked, "How did you do that?"

"Not in your pay grade, sweetheart." He reached out and collected the lamp and my camera then shoved them into my hands. Once the camera touched my flesh I felt immediate warmth. The deathly chill that I felt earlier dissipated, but my stomach began to gnaw away with hunger.

Vincent cocked his head to one side then took the power source and pocketed it. He marched back to where Mary laid on the floor and put his hands under her prone form.

"Um, what are you doing?"

He hefted Mary onto his shoulders like a duffle bag and started for the door. "Making sure our trouble maker doesn't have the opportunity to make things worse for us."

"Oh."

"Besides, I require payment for tonight's service." He gave a wry smile. "And she'll do."

Taking a page out of Mary's book, I replied with long drawn out vowels, "Oh, hell, no."

BEFORE I COULD REACH VINCENT, he vanished with Mary on his shoulder. Stupid, stupid, stupid. I pummeled the side of my head for not even considering that Vincent was playing at his own agenda tonight. The number one rule when dealing with demons is don't trust them.

Idiot me, put my trust in Vincent and got backstabbed. Yes, he did take the thorn in my side called Mary but she one-hundred percent did not deserve the hell he was going to give her. I walked over to the side table that was between the twin beds in the room and pulled out the drawer. Inside was a memo pad and a pencil. I grabbed both and scrawled a note for Ivan.

'Mary was taken by Vincent, a sex demon, who is one of Avarice's minions.

I don't know where she'll be but I'm sure you have a way of tracking each other.

Save her…

Oh, btw, I'm sorry I stole your truck, twice...
And stole back the artifacts.
Please forgive me.
~Sarah

My phone buzzed in my back pocket. How the darn thing didn't get destroyed from the many times I'd fallen on it was beyond me. I pulled it out and answered it. Glenda's voice purred.

"Tell me you have the artifact, dearie."

"Yes, I have *the* artifact. The lamp."

"Good. Now come meet me at the local cafe."

"Did you know that Vincent was going to take Mary?"

"Who?"

"Mary," I said through clenched teeth. "Did you know that Vincent was going to take her?"

"Dearie, I had no idea. What that demon does is his own thing. I may have agreed to such payment even if it happened to be you at a later date."

"What?" I yelled into the phone. "I thought you said I was yours. Was that a lie?"

"Yes, after tonight, if things go as planned then you would have been mine. But you do have a lot of debt following you around. There's no rule that says I could not make you pay your debts through certain services under my rule."

"You... bitch."

"Yes, I am one. Half-werewolf dearie. Kind of goes with the territory. Now stop dallying and get going," Glenda said and growled. "Don't make me hunt you down."

The call ended and I stood there breathing heavily through

my nose. The breathing exercises were not helping, and I felt my blood pressure spike. I threw the phone against the wall and yelled, "Argh."

The poor phone shattered to pieces and fell to the floor. I stomped out of the room, slammed the door behind me and headed towards where the driver waited for me at the other end of the lot. I got in and slammed the car door too.

"Lady, easy. You're gonna break my door doing that," the driver complained.

I glared at him. He held up his hands and said, "Whoa, sorry. Where to now?"

"The local cafe around the corner."

"You got it." He bobbed his head and put the car into gear. We went down the road for five minutes and pulled into the lot. To be fair I could have walked here but I didn't want to chance any zombies popping out of the ground and hijacking me to meet with Avarice earlier than intended.

I got out and paid the driver. He looked around the area, grimaced and took off. Guess he didn't like the vibes that hung around the place. It had an eerie vibe happening and the parking lot was near empty. In the shadows I saw something slink around in the forest that backed up to the cafe and the flash of gold fiery eyes.

Like the idiot that I was, I decided to go check it out.

CHAPTER
THIRTY

"WALTER?" I asked into the night shade of the forest. "You there?"

A twig snapped behind me and I jumped. From the shadow emerged the form of a seven-year-old boy with his hands in his pockets. His eyes narrowed while he looked me up and down.

"You are definitely not too bright."

"Hey."

"Well, it's true. If this was a horror movie you'd be dead by now," he replied as he circled around me like a shark.

"Can we stop with the dumb blonde jokes already?" I sighed and rubbed the bridge between my eyes. "I'm tired, hungry and just want to get this shit over with."

"Don't we all?"

"Why are you here?" I wasn't going to even ask how he got away from the dragon. He was a demon after all and they had many tricks at their disposal.

He quirked an eyebrow up and pouted. "You're not going to ask how I got away from the dragon? You're not a teensy bit concerned for my health or wellbeing?"

"Cut the crap, Seth." My stomach gurgled loudly. I wrapped my arm over it. "I'm really hungry right now and would love to go eat but I'm out here talking to you. As to why? I don't know. So, hurry up your demony spiel and we can both go our own ways."

He glanced at the lamp and camera that hung from my neck. Seth pursed his lips as he rocked back on his heels searching for his next words. His gaze landed on the tattoo on my right arm.

"I've a question for you." He pointed at my tattoo. "Did you ever notice that your tattoo stopped working the evening you used the camera on yourself?"

I frowned and looked down at my tattoo. What was he talking about? Upon further examination I noticed that the tattoo had not moved an inch from the time before. Like it had frozen or been deactivated.

My heart fluttered. I took in several deep breaths and sunk down to the ground wrapping my arms around my legs and placing my head between my knees. The tattoo, the number one thing that started all of this, could it have been deactivated?

Did that mean I was free? Free to rejoin the world of normalcy and ditch this supernatural world? I inhaled another deep breath, held it in and then released. Repeated the same breathing exercise to calm my racing heart.

"I'm guessing you've just now noticed based on your reaction," Seth said. "Too bad the camera now has a claim on your soul."

My head whipped up. "What?"

"You heard me." He snickered and pulled at the support strap that secured the camera. "That old piece of junk hanging from your neck now has you snared into a lifetime of servitude. Feed it life-forces or sacrifice your own. That is until you've completed all the tasks required."

"How do you know all this?"

"Duh." He rolled his eyes. "I'm a djinn. I know all sorts of things that hold other life-forces against their will."

"Okay smarty pants," I said. "What about *your* lamp? How come you're not bound to it?"

"I am."

"But how? You're not making any sense. How were you able to stay when Mary took it?"

"Don't hurt the hamster in the wheel Einstein."

"Oh ha, ha. Very funny. Mind telling me what's going on and why you're here then?"

He hunkered down in front of me and draped his arms over his knees. "I'm here for you. Since you have the lamp I have to come back to it eventually to regenerate my powers. I'm an elder and have a further range than most even though my form doesn't show my age."

"But back at Mrs. Smith's you said she didn't control you."

"That's still true."

I screwed up my face. Seth laughed and shook his head.

"Look, Sarah, do you still have that ring I gave you?"

I nodded and reached into my pocket, pulled it out and held it out to him. The gold gleamed in the moonlight. Seth picked it up and examined it.

"Too bad you didn't call on me earlier to help with your friend. I would have come."

Massaging my temple I let out another sigh. "I'm done with magic and riddles. Besides, I thought you gave me a fake artifact which is why I didn't use it. Now you're telling me that the trinket would have worked?"

Seth nodded and handed it back. "Yes, but don't worry about that anymore. Instead, I want you to do something else with it."

"Like, what?"

"That ring is far more valuable than my lamp or even that camera. It has a glamor applied to it and I was entrusted to hold onto it until now."

I shifted on the ground to move away from the stick poking me in the butt. With my legs crossed, I sat up with the ring in my left hand and kept a good eye on Seth.

He continued, "Yes, this seems all stupid and I probably sound like the stupid *'You're the chosen one'* trope but that's the thing... you are. With this ring, if you remove the lens on your camera and insert the ring into the lens mount, that will increase the camera's power."

"And what good will that do?"

"You'll have the power to control demons. It's the reason why Mrs. Smith never had control over me because I possessed this particular ring artifact. Or you may know it as Solomon's ring."

My jaw dropped and hung open long enough for bugs to fly in. Seth reached over and used his finger under my chin to close my mouth. I'd heard of Solomon's ring. Always thought of it as a myth. Times like tonight reminded me that in the magical world, myths, legends and fairy tales were real.

"So you're saying that I'll have control over you if I combine the ring with the camera? Will that even work? And why would you want to do this?"

He gestured for me to commence with the process of removing the lens from the camera. "Let's just say that I don't want to be in Avarice's hands… again."

My eyes bugged out.

"Will you stop stalling?" he said. "I doubt it will be long before that she-wolf comes out here to look for your sorry behind. Do you want her to get ahold of Solomon's ring? Or even have control over me?"

"No." I shook my head. My fingers shook as I brought the ring close to the exposed lens mount. I licked my lips and squinted my eyes shut and tapped the ring to the exposed metal.

Part of me expected a bright flash or some other blast of magnificent powers. Especially when combining two great artifacts with one another. But, there was none. Instead, the ring melted and oozed around the lens mount and solidified. The camera took on a different hum. Taking the lens I placed it back over the mount and clicked it back onto the case.

Seth watched the entire process and said nothing while the process unfolded before us both. He nodded once more with a calm demeanor and pointed at himself. "Okay, now take my picture."

"What?" I nearly choked on saliva. "Are you crazy?"

"No. Just take my picture."

"But you'll die," I argued.

He rolled his eyes and let out a sigh. "Trust me, take my picture."

"Ha, I learned my lesson about trusting demons. No."

"You're running out of time." Seth looked towards the cafe when we both heard doors open and close. "I promise nothing bad will happen."

"Fine," I grumbled and held up the camera. Of course, I shut my eyes. My finger slid over the shutter button and pressed it down. The audible click sounded, followed by a flash.

"You can open your eyes now." Seth still sat across from me in all his snarky glory.

I brought the camera down and asked, "You're not going to die now, are you?"

"No."

"But I thought this camera stole lifeforces. Why won't yours be taken?"

"Because of the ring."

I got up and rolled my shoulders. Dusted myself off and offered a hand to Seth. "I'm just going to roll with it. I'm too tired and hungry to continue trying to wrap my poor brain around all this mumbo jumbo 'chosen one' crap."

He grabbed ahold of my hand and pulled himself up off the ground. "It's the ring that allowed my service to be transferred to this camera instead of the lamp. And the ring ensures that the camera doesn't devour my essence."

"But why me?"

"I like you. Isn't that obvious? I threw the riddle game for you." He smiled.

"Uh, thanks, I guess."

Crickets chirped in the darkness. I lifted the lamp that hung from a chain with my pinky and examined it. "So, you're now saying the lamp is useless? Will they know?"

"The lamp will work for a few days with shadows of my essence. After those days are up then the lamp is rendered useless. Just hope that Glenda or Avarice don't wish for something crazy during that time or we'll be in big trouble."

"Got it." I bobbed my head and turned towards the cafe. "Guess it's time for me to go talk with Glenda. You coming?"

No answer. I turned to find that Seth was gone. Where'd he go?

CHAPTER
THIRTY-ONE

THE GROUND RUMBLED and shifted as Walter rose up from underneath and stood before me. His arms crossed over his chest and glared down at me.

"Hey Walter." I tucked my hair behind my ear. "What's the occasion?"

"You need to stop," he said in a low gravelly voice. "Stop this ridiculousness with my mother and come with me. Avarice wants to talk, now."

"No. I promised your mother this lamp, she's getting this lamp."

"I saw you earlier with that djinn." He narrowed his eyes. "Don't think you'll fool my mother with that broken artifact."

"She won't know." I stepped onto the asphalt of the parking lot.

"My mother isn't stupid. Unlike someone else I know," Walter replied.

I swung around and poked him in his squishy chest. "Gawd, you too? I thought you'd be the only one who didn't call me stupid every five seconds."

"I'm not apologizing," he quipped. "You know, deep down, that what you're doing is a hare-brained scheme that is only going to get you killed."

"I'm dead already." I hung my head. "Doesn't matter what I do now."

"Sarah," he whispered as he brushed the side of my face and tucked the loose strands of hair behind my ear.

"I've got to go."

"Please, don't."

"Walter, I have to…" my eyes became moist as my voice cracked, "for your sake."

His hand dropped down and he stepped back to his hole. He took one more look and worry filled his milky white eyes. He let out a long sigh before he said, "As you wish."

I blew him a kiss one last time before he sunk back into the ground.

The world felt lonelier now and I wasn't one-hundred percent sure that I was truly going to pull this off and get him back. It felt like this was my last true moment with Walter and this was our good-bye. I had lost him.

Wiping the tears away from my eyes I turned back around, ensured the artifacts were still on my person and headed for the cafe. Let's go see if I can fool a half-werewolf.

AS PER THE parking lot predicted the cafe was near empty. Glenda was situated in the far back with a plate of eaten chicken wings piled high to one side and another she was currently devouring. At least she won't be too hungry to eat me tonight, I hoped.

Glenda waved at me and snapped her fingers at the barista to make a few lattes for us both. I slid into the seat opposite to her and said, "I have your artifact."

A chicken wing midway to her mouth hung limp in her hand as her yellow eyes snapped to me. She dropped the wing onto the plate, used a napkin to clean her hands of the barbecue sauce and reached out. "Show me."

I pulled the chain that the lamp hung on up out of my shirt and over my head then placed it on the table. Glenda snatched it up and looked it over, hemming and hawing. I sat there chewing on my fingernails while acid swirled inside my innards. The half-werewolf whose nails looked more like claws tonight clicked and tapped over the lamp before she rubbed it.

Please, please, please work. I was on the verge of throwing up while we sat there waiting on a response from the lamp. Glenda stared me down and tapped her claws on the table. A low growl emanated from the woman. Crap, why was it not working? Crap, crap, crap.

Glenda rubbed the lamp again but with more vigor this time. She snarled while she rubbed, "Don't think you can fool me, Sarah. If you've tried to swap this with a fake then it's your spine I will take."

Eep.

A golden mist spurted from the lamp in sparks. Glenda smiled and rubbed harder to coax the genie out from within. The mist flowed into the room and gathered onto the floor like the mist from dry ice. More mist combined and built upon itself until the form of a seven-year-old boy stood before us.

"How may I serve you, master?" Seth said.

"Seth?" I asked.

"In a way, yes," Seth-not-seth replied. He moved back to Glenda and bowed with a flourish, "Master, how may I serve thee tonight?"

Glenda's lips split into a wicked smile that showed her sharp elongated teeth. "It is good to see you once more dearie."

"Time, indeed, has passed since we last met," Seth-not-seth said. "Is there something that you wish, master?"

The half-werewolf shook her head and said, "No. You are dismissed for now."

Seth-not-seth bowed and dissipated into the gold mist. The mist lifted from the floor and siphoned back into the lamp that Glenda held in her hands. She patted it then pushed it off to one side. A twinkle in her yellow eyes told me that she was either pleased or she was about to swallow me whole. You could never truly tell with wolves.

"For once, you did good, dearie," she cooed then picked up the chicken wing to gnaw on the bones and flesh.

An unnerving sensation in the pit of my stomach flipped several times. And the hairs on the back of my neck rose. I should leave now. Something didn't feel right. I clutched onto the camera and felt a reassuring tingle rush through me.

Glenda eyed the camera in my hands and asked, "Is that *the* camera?"

"Yes." I held it closer. "It's mine."

"Good," she crooned and dabbed a napkin to her lips. "I wanted to make sure that you brought all the artifacts here tonight."

"You're not getting my camera," I argued and pulled away in my chair. "That wasn't part of our deal."

"No, not ours." She turned to the back darkened doorway. "But mine."

The chill rushed down my spine again and I shivered. I really should leave, now.

"Oh, would you look at the time?" I said while I got up from my chair.

Glenda lunged and grabbed my wrist before I could bolt. She patted my hand and said, "No, stay, please, I insist."

She turned back to the darkened doorway. My danger meter

screamed that things had gone south and crashed badly and was on fire with no way in hell of escape. A familiar shadow came forward and lingered before stepping out into the room.

Glenda chirped, "Oh Avarice, you came."

CHAPTER
THIRTY-THREE

THE FLOOR CAME out from under me and I sank down to my knees. Glenda clenched my wrist so tight in her grasp that the circulation was cut off. I felt ready to puke as the room spun around me and I needed fresh air. Glenda refused to release her iron grip as I yanked my arm.

Avarice sashayed into the room. The horde of zombies shuffled in the back and waited for her command. Six-inch heels clicked on the floor with each step she took towards our table. She placed a hand on Glenda's shoulder and looked down at me with an imperious smile.

"My, my, my, Sarah," Avarice said. "You've been busy."

Her elegant fingers with well manicured fingernails reached over on the table and picked up the lamp. Glenda let a low growl rumble and Avarice paused.

"Now, Glenda, I'll have none of that. Be a good dog and don't cause a fuss."

Yellow flared brighter in Glenda's eyes before she turned her head away. Her hand, still with a vice grip around my poor wrist. I coughed and said, "Can I have my hand back, please?"

Avarice arched an eyebrow and said, "Glenda? Drop it. Now."

Glenda growled again.

"Glenda, behave."

My mother-in-law let go of my hand, huffed and turned her back on us. Avarice's smile faded while she continued her inspection of the lamp. Her eyes scrutinized the artifact and she placed it back on the table.

"This is defective," she said.

Glenda whirled back around, eyes wide, and sputtered. She said, "No, I checked the lamp before I called you in here. I promise you that it works."

Avarice's frown deepened. "The genie is no longer there. What you saw was his shade which will dissipate in three days."

"But, but, but—" Glenda said.

Avarice placed her finger on Glenda's lips and cut her off. "Enough. I'm not really here for the lamp. If it was an active lamp then it would have been a boon for me."

The half-werewolf breathed a sigh of relief. My heart pounded when Avarice looked straight down at me. "I'm here for Sarah, whom you promised to deliver to me. And you have."

I felt faint and I had no energy to move. Avarice bent down and glanced at the camera that I held in my hands. "And what do we have here?"

She pried the camera from my hands, which wasn't too hard since I was as weak as a newborn kitten and turned it over in hers. The wry smile returned to her lips as she caressed the body of the camera. "Mmm, what did you bring me, my sweet? This feels powerful. Very powerful."

"I-i-it's mine," I said and shivered. The camera was out of my grasp for a mere second and I was starting to feel cold again. Chills crawled up and down my spine.

"No," Avarice replied. "It's mine."

With one last effort I lunged to take the camera from her grasp but she moved out of my way and I fell forward onto my face. My body became wracked with sudden shakes that prevented me from standing up. I curled into a fetal position to try and keep what warmth I still had.

"Interesting," Avarice said and toed my shuddering form on the ground. I watched her expensive heels walk away towards the back room.

Reaching out I said, "Wait."

She paused and waited.

"Give me back my camera," I said between chills. "I need it."

"And why would I do that Sarah?"

"I'll die."

"Not my problem." She turned away and called for her goons.

Intense cold engulfed my entire being, my heart rate slowed and my fingers became numb. I stuttered between chattering teeth, "P-p-please."

Glenda stepped into view and bent down. She growled, "Shut up. I'll never see what my son saw in you. You've been nothing but a pain since you came into his life. I'll be glad when you get what's coming to you."

Avarice called back, "Leave the frozen worm to her own demise, Glenda. I'll deal with her in a moment. Besides, I believe you wanted to discuss the payment of our deal, am I correct?"

"Yes." Glenda jumped up, whined and clasped her hands together. "My son, for the artifacts and one traitor."

"Ah, of course." Avarice purred and snapped her fingers. From the back Walter shambled into the front room. The light beamed down on his decomposing form and dirty clothing. Glenda let out an ear shattering shriek and fainted.

THIRTY-FOUR

AVARICE NODDED to her two non-zombie goons to pick up Glenda and escort her out of the cafe. She snapped her fingers for Walter to follow his mother as well. The rest of the zombie horde waited in the back. Their moans became more frenzied the longer they were kept at bay.

The camera swayed in front of me on its strap. Avarice asked, "Where did you get this camera?"

"P-p-pawn shop," I stuttered and hunched more into myself. Warmth was escaping my being faster than I could create it. If only I could snatch the camera out of Avarice's grasp to regain the warmth and to stop it from stealing my life-force.

She pursed her lips and tapped her chin. "Interesting. Did the shop have the initials WoV on it?"

"Y-y-yeah," I said between chattering teeth. "It did."

"Hmmm, now, that makes sense."

"W-w-what makes sense?"

"Don't worry your pretty little head about it." She lifted my chin. Her fingers felt nice and warm. "Where you're going you won't have to worry about this camera or about deadlines ever again. You'll make a wonderful zombie, Sarah."

Well, I did say that this was one of the outcomes. Either the camera would suck the rest of my life-force away, zombie hordes would devour me or I ended up as a new zombie minion.

"A-a-and Walter?" I asked. "What about him?"

"Walter?" Avarice replied and laughed. "He's been released and returned to his dear old mumsy. Though he will require a resurrection spell to undo the damage. He'll make a full recovery to the living, my dear."

She clapped her hands twice and zombies shambled into the room. She pointed down at my prone form and said, "Bring her."

Two of the zombies near the front groaned and shuffled to where I laid and grabbed me. One helped bring me upright and placed me in the open arms of the other zombie. It wrapped its arms around my shaking body and held tight.

Avarice led the horde outside and the one that held me tight to its fetid form came to a stop once its feet touched dirt. Avarice motioned with her hands and said to the horde, "Return, my darlings, until you are called upon once more."

She gestured to the rotting zombie that held me in place and added, "Take that one to the changing chambers."

The ground beneath our feet shifted and we sunk down into the dirt. I screamed and tried to claw my way out of the undead creature's grasp but was held tight. Its grip unrelenting. The world was swallowed up around me as my screams were muffled by the dirt that slowly covered the hole. Darkness enveloped me and only the sound of my own racing heart told me there was no use struggling. I felt each thud become heavier with every beat while my own lungs burned for air.

There was no escape now. I was so screwed.

WATER DRIPPED IN THE BACKGROUND. The ground was cool and hard underneath my cheek. I patted around with my hand while I still had my eyes closed. Smooth cold surface, well worn in areas, I felt with my fingertips. It was weird that I could feel the cold floor given that not long ago I was shivering up a storm.

"About time," Teddy said. "Thought you'd never wake up."

"Teddy?" I rose up, squinted and gingerly rubbed the back of my head. Dirt scattered to the floor as I ran my fingers through my hair.

"The one and only," he replied and bent forward, the old wooden bench creaked that he sat upon, just above where I lay on the ground. His clothing was torn and shredded. Days of dirt and unmentionables clung to the material and added to the ambience of the room.

"What are you doing here?"

He raked his fingers through his greasy unkempt hair. His other hand sought out phantom glasses that were no longer resting on his nose. "After you took off, mister sex demon decided to take his anger out on yours truly."

"What? Why?"

"I dunno." He shrugged his shoulders. "Maybe he thought he could lure you back with me? He's an idiot if he thought he could."

"I'm sorry." I frowned.

Teddy wrapped his arms around his chest and shuddered. One of his hands, the right one, was missing fingers, an index and part of the middle finger. Dark circles framed his eyes just above his swollen broken nose. He talked in a low whisper. "He did things to me, Sarah. Things that I never ever wanted to even explore in my entire life."

"Aw, Teddy." I reached for his knee but he pulled away.

"Don't touch me." Teddy's voice cracked. He sniffed but could not hold back the silent tears. "I told you that I didn't want your nonsense brought to my doorstep. But you and Walter did it anyway."

"I never meant—"

"But you did." Teddy cut me off. He stared me down, his eyes hard and unforgiving. "You and your shitty husband both knew what kind of danger you were bringing to my turf but you did not give a shit. Instead you both trasped around willy nilly not even hiding your tracks about breaking the spell on those stupid tattoos. Oh, let's not worry about our friends or that they might become collateral if things go sideways."

Silence held my tongue, and I sat there letting Teddy continue.

"Do you know what that sex fiend did after you left?"

I shook my head.

"He set my motel on fire." He yelled and pounded the wood with his hand. "Everything that I held dear… poof… gone. All because I was doing you and Walter a solid. What a fucking mistake that was… I should have shot both of you when you came knocking and asking for help."

Water dripped. There must have been a leaky pipe somewhere. I bit my bottom lip, unsure of what to say to Teddy. He was beaten, tortured and raped. His motel business was gone. All because Walter and I didn't care who got caught in the crosshairs of our stupid scheme to break free of the supernatural mafia.

A lump of guilt lodged itself in my throat but I swallowed it to ask, "Have you seen anyone else brought here?"

"Besides you?" he asked, then shook his head. "No."

"How long have I been out?"

"Only a few hours. Some rather gnarly looking guards that smelled riper than expired feta cheese threw you in here while you were unconscious." He sighed. "I've been here for days."

"Where are we, exactly?"

"Beats me." He huffed and rubbed his arms. "I have no clue. All I know is that we're in some holding cell. The guards keep talking about some big ceremony."

"Ceremony?"

"Yeah."

"Did they say what it was going to be about?"

Teddy wiped the front of his face and replied, "Something about zombification, dead rites or something. Didn't care to listen since it doesn't matter anymore. I'm as good as dead anyways."

"Seriously? Teddy, you're always the one for details."

"Did I fucking stutter? It doesn't matter anymore. My choices are, continue being the experimental sex slave to your demon sex fiend or die. I'm choosing death. Death is a better alternative to the seven hells of sexual torture."

I held up my hands. "Okay, okay. Got it. I'm sorry I asked."

Footsteps sounded outside the old wooden cell door. Men grumbled as they handled their new prisoner. One cried out, "Ow. She kicked me."

Another said, "Keep a hold of her better or you're going in there with them."

The woman's reply was muffled by a gag of some sort.

"Ow," the first man cried out again. "She almost got me jewels on that one."

"Do ye have her now?" the second guard said to the third. "Are ye sure?"

"Yes," third guard said but obviously struggled with his prisoner. "She's a feisty one."

Metal on metal scraped when the lock on our cell door clicked open. The guards shoved the door open, first guard held his gun at the ready, second held the door open and the third threw his captive into the room. The second guard swung the door shut before the woman on the floor had a chance to pounce.

It slammed in her face, and she banged on the door as she shouted, "Oh, hell, no, you ain't stuffing me in no dank dungeon to be forgotten about. I demand to talk to your superiors. Parley you fucking morons. I said fucking parley. Don't you dolts know the meaning of that word?"

She was a sight for sore eyes. The last I saw of her was when Vincent took her as payment for his help. Her spirit was certainly not broken even if her hair and clothes were more ragged from the rough fighting she had earlier on.

The door rattled on its hinges when she delivered a swift kick. She turned and slumped to the ground and laid her arms over her knees. A deep sigh escaped her lips while she hung her head.

"Mary?" I said.

Mary snapped her head up then narrowed her eyes. Immediately she jumped back up and banged on the door while calling out to the guards. "Guards. Guards. You need to move me. I cannot be in here with this other person. There will be blood."

The first guard yelled back, "Shad'up."

"I'm serious," Mary shouted. "I will kill this woman if you do not move me to another cell."

Another guard replied, "So? Like we care if you kill each other or not. Boss don't care either."

"Are you sure?"

"Look lady," second guard said. "I don't give a rat's ass if you chop off her legs and stuff 'em down her throat. Just as long as you do it quietly then that's fine by me. Boss can zombify anything so it won't matter."

Mary banged on the door again. "Damnit."

Teddy sat on the bench with wide eyes and looked between us. He asked me, "You know her?"

"Yeah." I tucked a loose strand of hair behind my ear. "Kind of…"

Mary whirled back around, grabbed the front of my shirt and slammed me against the wall. "Ain't no kind of. You blondie have been the bane of my existence ever since I put eyes on you back at the gas station. If only Ivan never picked your sorry ass up then things would have turned out differently."

The bench creaked when Teddy got up and walked over to Mary. He placed his hand on her arm and said, "Let her go. I know you're hurting but let her go. Killing her won't make what happened go away."

"This bitch," Mary said with tears in her eyes as she turned to Teddy, "this bitch started all of this bullshit. I've never met someone who causes as much harm as she has… if I never met her then I would never have to… never had to…"

Her hand released the hold on my shirt and I slid down the wall. Mary sunk down to the ground and Teddy followed her while he rubbed her back. He talked in soothing tones and whispered words to her.

"You know her?" I asked Teddy. "You both… um… were with Vincent?"

"The sex demon?" Mary's eyes filled with fire. "That unholy beast that *you* associate with?"

"Calm down Mary." Teddy rubbed her back.

"No." She swiped at Teddy's hand, stood and walked to the other end of the room. "She needs to understand what that maniac did… to me… to both of us. She *needs* to know that it's her fault."

Teddy opened his mouth then closed it. Silence filled the

room except for the sound of the water dripping from the leaky pipe. Outside the guards busted out with raucous laughter, playing a round of cards and complaining to one another about how bad their luck was that night.

Both Teddy and Mary were here because of me. If I had not tried to swindle my way out of the mafia by trying to disenchant the tattoo then these two would not be in line to become more zombie slaves. Mary was right. The sheer thought sent heart palpitations through me. I was scum.

"You're right," I said. "Neither of you would be here if it weren't for me."

"Damn straight," Mary replied.

"I agree with Mary," Teddy added. "I wish I'd never met you Sarah. My life would certainly be a lot better if you and your damn husband never showed up at my door."

Jeez. Talk about layering on the guilt. Here I was baring my soul and the two went on ahead and dog-piled the 'feel bad' feeling to add onto the crushing pressure. I was trying to make good here, people.

"You know what?" I said. "I take it all back. Fuck you and you. I'm not sorry that life served you a shit sandwich and you were forced to eat it. Plenty of people end up eating shit sandwiches every single day of their entire lives."

"Fuck your shit sandwich," Mary spat. "I didn't order it and I refuse to eat it."

I stomped my foot and pointed at myself. "I was a victim too. I never wanted to be in the supernatural mafia but I was dragged kicking and screaming."

Mary and Teddy blinked. The two stood and waited for me to continue.

"Why do you think I wanted out so bad?" I said to the room in general. "I really wanted to be a photographer but stupid me ordered the shit sandwich instead. And here we are…"

"Shit sandwich central," Teddy smirked. "So, we can either choose to eat our shitty sandwiches or should we devise an escape plan?"

Mary looked between us then sucked air in between her teeth. She placed her hands on her hips and said, "Well, I ain't eating no shit sandwich tonight nor do I plan on doing it anytime soon. I'm game for figuring out a way out of here."

I bobbed my head, clapped my hands together and rubbed them. "I'm all for that. Any differences or grievances we have we'll just put them aside until we get out."

"Fine with me," Teddy said and went over to the doors. He examined the hinges and the latches looking for any weak spots. Mary scanned the room seeking out any other potential escape routes. I listened for the water and followed it to the other corner of the cell.

The two paused what they were doing and watched when I stopped at the wall and tried to scale it. The walls were high and difficult to climb. I pointed up where the wall faded into the vast darkness. "The dripping sound of water is coming from up there. Can either one of you give me a boost?"

Mary came over and shoved me aside. "Move it blondie. Let the pros handle this bit."

She took a few steps back and ran at the wall then used the opposing wall as leverage to bounce between the two to climb up to the top. Her hand snatched out and grabbed a hold of the ledge before she lost her footing.

"Hey, there's a hole up here," she called down to us in a raspy whisper, too low for the guards down the hallway to hear. I kept my ears perked for them to barge into the room.

Mary continued, "I think I can wiggle on through it."

Teddy rose up on his toes and asked, "Do you think you can wiggle through and go get help?"

"Maybe." Mary pulled herself up onto the ledge. She lay on her stomach and crawled forward then stopped. She said, "Yeah. I'll fit."

Mary started forward again when Teddy called out, "Wait."

She paused and replied, "Don't worry. I'll go get help. Promise."

Teddy nodded, went back to the bench and sat down. He repeated to himself as he hugged his knee, "We're good now. Things are going to get better. Help is on the way. Help is coming."

I shouted, "You better come back."

"Shut up blondie. I've got this..." Mary said while she crawled deeper into the hole and hopefully to freedom. Part of me wanted to believe that she would go get help. The other part knew that even if help came it would be too late.

I leaned up against the wall and let out a dramatic sigh. There was no telling when the zombification ceremony was going to happen. Out of habit I brought my hands to blow into them when I noticed that the ends of my fingertips were turning black. Was I turning into a zombie? Was that why I no longer shivered?

Metal on metal clanged and clicked, breaking my thoughts,

before the old wooden door scraped open. On the other side stood the three guards with one of my least favorite people, Vincent. The first guard peered in and asked, "Where'd the other one go?"

I looked him in the eye and said, "I ate her."

The guard jumped back and gripped his gun tighter. He said to Vincent, "I guess they killed one another."

"Did they now?" Vincent smirked and entered the room. His eyes searched the cell and narrowed on the far corner. He pointed at the wall and said, "She must have escaped."

"Impossible," the second guard said. "No one can scale these walls. I believe the lady over there, that she must have eaten her."

Vincent grabbed the guard and shook him. "Moron. A prisoner has escaped. Take your men and go catch her or Avarice will have *more* bodies to convert into zombies tonight."

The three guards stumbled as they grabbed their gear and ran to alert the other guards about the escapee. Bells rang out while more guards snapped to attention and started searching. I only hoped that Mary got a good head start on her escape before those idiots could catch her.

Vincent snapped at one of the guards, "Bring those two down below to the chambers. We're getting ready and they're our VIPs for the night."

CHAPTER
THIRTY-SIX

THEY LED us down two more levels before we entered the chamber through grand archways that reached high into the cavernous ceilings. All of the supernatural mafia's base was built into natural cave systems. Lighting lit small bits and lost against the war of keeping the darkness at bay. There were stations that were placed under each pooling of light. Pathways were lit by fluorescent mushrooms that edged the worn smooth cobblestones that dictated the flow of traffic.

Goblins and bat-like creatures scurried around the room grabbing things needed at their designated stations. Fights broke out between the creatures with zombies called forth to broker peace or make the offenders into bloody pieces on the ground.

Our living guard shuddered when he watched a zombie close by go berserk on an unsuspecting bat-like creature. Sheer chaos filled the room. You'd think that with a ceremony there would be more order in play. But no, there was nothing that indicated that something big was about to happen. It all felt like this was the normal day to day.

Teddy leaned in close. "Psst. What do you think is going on here?"

"The normal day to day?" I shrugged. "The way I see it we're not really the VIPs tonight."

What was happening around us certainly did not feel special at all. Did the supernatural mafia turn out zombie slaves on a normal basis? I kind of felt insulted by the sheer thought that my zombification was going to be treated as normal. I snorted and shook my head. Normal, yeah right. I wanted normal right? Right? Guess I was getting my wish... no matter how twisted it ended up being.

"Keep moving." Vincent shoved my shoulder. "We've got a schedule to keep sweetheart."

I stumbled but regained my footing. The guard yanked on the rope pulling Teddy and myself along the pathway. We hurried as fast as we could walk with the gang-chain hindering our steps.

From other archways more captives entered, their faces grim and desolate. Many appeared to have been here for several weeks. They too were led across the room to the center where three large pillars rose up into the dark and sported at least eight to ten chains for holding unwilling victims. The unholy columns of granite emitted negative energy that caused the hairs on the back of my neck to stand on end.

Prisoners who got closer bucked, screamed and refused to move closer. Some were tearing their hair out if pushed toward the center of evil. Others wet themselves while some relieved their bowels due to the sheer terror that came off in waves from the columns. Guards, in various species - orcs, humans, ogres, prodded the unwilling humans to stand up and be manacled. Screams of anguish and pleas for their pitiful lives blanketed the cavern.

By the look of numerous unfortunate souls before us, I estimated that Teddy and I were to be part of the fifth wave. Bored looking goblins held staves with blood-red crystals gathered around each column and danced around mumbling in words not meant for human mouths. Watching them reminded me of a demented dance of ring around the rosies, of course that song was morbid in of itself. The goblins shifted right, then left, held their staves in the air and waved them in a clockwise motion and stamped them on the ground. Then they reversed the motion. After they did the motion three times, the word, 'Zombie,' echoed through the cavern as they thudded their staves in a final move.

Acrid, thick smoke snaked up through the holes in the ground around the columns. The people began screaming while the mist crawled up their flesh, leaving necrotic flesh behind. When the fog completely swallowed the poor souls the cavern became silent before the long drawn out moan issued forth from the new zombie slaves.

The goblins unshackled the new recruits and hustled them off to one side. Guards used whips to crowd control the zombies down another tunnel. They groaned for brains as they shambled down the corridor and out of sight. Their transformation way different from Walter's transformation. The whole situation here spoke volumes that Avarice had different tiers of zombies. Walter was considered a high tier whereas here, were the bottom of the barrel type of zombie minions.

Our line of unfortunates moved up. I silently prayed for Mary or someone to come to our rescue or even for the camera to suck the last bit of my life-force away. Yes, I had this coming, but I certainly did not want to become a zombie.

Ghouls, orcs, goblins, bat-like creatures, ogres and more continued business as normal. They pulled and yanked people into place and strapped them in. Another wave became zombies by the red flash of death.

Two more waves before our time was up. If Mary was about to pull off a miraculous rescue then right now would be good. Heck, I would even welcome an attack from the dragon if that meant it delayed my zombification or even allowed me to escape.

A goblin hobbled up to me and Teddy. He motioned for me to bend down and held his hand up to the side to hide his words from the others. The goblin asked, "Are you Sarah Knight?"

Unsure, I worried my bottom lip but answered, "Yes. That's me. Why?"

"Come." He undid our shackles and motioned for us to follow. "I've been told to bring you."

Teddy leaned into me and asked, "What's he want?"

"He wants us to follow him."

"And you think that's a good idea?"

"Better than standing in line to be turned in a zombie." I glanced at the guard whose attention was turned elsewhere.

"Ah, good point."

The goblin hopped up and down, beckoning with his hands for us to follow. "Come, come. You must hurry."

Teddy and I both shrugged our shoulders and followed the little green man as he shambled on all four across the uneven floor between the pathways. Our absence went unnoticed. My stomach still did somersaults as we got further from the path and followed the creature to an unknown destination.

The goblin paused and waited for us to catch up. "Come, not far now."

You'd think the other creatures in the room would take notice of two humans running free of the queue to zombieville but none stopped us. Which is why the sick sensation ratcheted up a notch in my belly.

Teddy stopped. He looked at the goblin and then back at the line. His lips worried into a thin line. I could tell he was feeling unsure of our choice to follow this creature. Teddy said, "I dunno. This feels kind of off. My gut is telling me things are about to get way worse."

"I know how you feel," I replied and rubbed my stomach. "But I'd prefer the unknown instead of becoming a zombie. Sorry, but that's how I feel. You can go back if you want but I want to see what our little goblin friend has in store for us."

The goblin crawled back to us and pulled on my hand. He said in an enthusiastic voice, "Come, yes, come. Not far, not far. You'll see."

"Hey little guy, where are you taking us?" I said and bent at the knees.

"You'll see," he replied. "Come."

I looked back at Teddy and followed after the goblin that scurried ahead of us. Teddy followed but continued to look back over his shoulder at the queue of unfortunate souls. He let out a shuddered breath and worked his short legs to keep up.

"This feels bad, Sarah," Teddy puffed. "Real bad."

"I know," was all I said and picked up the pace. The goblin paused periodically to make sure that we were following him to a far off corner within the cavern. His yellow eyes reflected the light from the room and glowed in the dark. Eerie little son-of-a-gun.

We caught up and he led us into a hidden tunnel where we stood in the dark. The only light coming from the goblin's yellow eyes. Teddy hummed to himself while we waited.

A lone pebble ricocheted off the tunnel walls followed by the sound of footsteps. The person or creature tried to be quiet, but the stone gave their presence away.

"Hello?" I said into the dark. "Anyone there?"

Whispers sounded in the dark and the goblin replied in low whispers as well. The person cleared their throat and said, "Oh, hell, that was easier than I thought."

Mary. Our mysterious person was Mary. What the hell was she doing down here instead of going for help? Ugh. She's going to get caught and end up as a zombie too.

"What the fuck are you doing down here?" I hissed. "Aren't you supposed to be getting the calvary or something?"

"Blondie, there are these things called phones, y'know the objects that enable communication from afar without physically needing to go to that destination. You should check them out sometime," she said and mumbled under her breath, "Jeez, I swear, you're such an idiot."

"But I thought you were escaping to go get help. Not come back here to try and save us." I fired back at her.

"Did I stutter?" She bared her perfectly white teeth. "I got out, found an unattended phone, called Ivan, who is gathering all of Wings of Virtue to come save our asses. He asked me to try and save the both of you."

"Oh."

"Yeah, oh." She replied with heavy snark.

The goblin piped in before I could give Mary a tongue lashing. "I did good? Reward I get?"

"Indeed. Here ya go. As promised one can of delicious sardines."

I'm not going to ask where she got a can of sardines. Not going to even ask. The sound of metal being pried open by sharp talons followed by loud slurps sent chills down my spine. Ick. The goblin noshed on his reward before he tossed the tin away, it pinged off the wall, and he scrambled out of the tunnel.

"So what's the plan now?" I asked. "Hunker down here until the cavalry comes?"

"No. We have to move. Come on." She grabbed our arms before we could protest and led us deeper into the tunnel. Our feet tripped over unseen stones and bumps in the path.

We continued on down the dark tunnel until a light shone at the end. Mary stopped and said, "Stay here while I check to make sure the coast is clear."

I nodded and sat back while she went off to verify that no one was waiting for us to pop out into the room considering that all the guards were on alert for an escapee. After five minutes Mary leaned in and waved for us to follow her. Teddy and I shuffled our feet in the dark and squinted our eyes against the light.

The room was a small storage room with supplies like blankets, food, potable water and more. A box beside the tunnel was already torn into and displayed the labels of sardines. No mystery on where she got the tin of smelly fish now.

Teddy stepped forward and tried to push glasses that weren't there up his nose. He asked, "Now what?"

Mary was moving about the room looking through boxes for something. She ripped into one and pulled out clothing. They appeared to be uniforms. She examined Teddy and sifted through the box before she pulled out another set of pants which she tossed over to him.

Teddy snatched the clothing out of the air. He didn't hesitate to change out of his rags into clothing that offered more coverage and the potential of blending in. Mary threw clothing and they sideswiped my face.

I grumbled but picked them off the floor and changed into them too while she searched for shoes. Mary found them and pulled out two pairs of black combat boots. One for Teddy and the other for me. We grabbed and put them on.

With the hats in place we could blend in easier and perhaps this nightmare before they even knew we left the queue. We were all clad in the supernatural mafia's guard uniforms. Mary clapped her hands. "Okay, now that y'all are suited up, let's get the fuck out of here."

"What about all those people down there?" Teddy asked. "We can't leave them."

"Oh we're leaving them." I pushed Teddy forward. "They

knew what they were signing up for when they agreed to the terms."

Teddy stopped and turned around. "Like you did?"

Ohh, low blow Teddy. Real low. Mary let out a low whistle in surprise at Teddy's comeback. I stood there, blinked several times with my mouth hung open, then closed and opened it again. He was right.

Luckily, Mary swooped in and said, "Look, I've got a whole swat team coming down on this area and they'll handle the poor schmucks that were stupid enough to sign such agreements. I promise."

"Right." I nodded and smiled back at Mary. "So, let's go."

Teddy looked between us, sighed and pushed through to the door. As he opened the door a high pitched alarm went off and sent waves that turned the world on its side. One moment I was standing and the next the floor was rushing up to meet my face. Mary and Teddy both stared at me as I laid on the ground and convulsed.

My whole being felt like it was suddenly immersed into arctic ice water. I screamed while my muscles contracted into painful contortions. Any normal warmth that I felt was gone.

Teddy yelled, "What's wrong with her?"

"Shit." Mary tore at one of her nails. She let the door slam close and bent down, her hands seeking all over for the potential cause. As she patted my lower back something clinked. She shoved me over and said, "Hold her down."

Teddy pressed my shoulders down while Mary shoved my shirt up to examine my lower back. She let out a curse and tapped the object again. "Well, shit. Either I leave it and let this stupid thing continue to send Blondie into series of convulsions or we risk yanking it off and potentially letting her go paralyzed."

"What is it?" Teddy asked and pressed harder on my shoulders. "How big is the risk?"

"Eh, I think maybe a sixty forty chance of her getting damaged. But this thing here is what was cutting off her connection to the camera. Probably needed it to allow the zombification to happen."

Teddy gasped. "Do I have one?"

"No. Only Blondie due to her connection with the cursed camera."

"Cursed camera?" he said. "I don't remember her having a camera. When did she get that?"

"About two days ago at a pawn shop. I should have bought it before she could. The camera steals the life-force of the owner. Which is why each camera owner only lasts seven days max, some less than that, unless they knew how to offset the camera's hunger."

"Good lord, Sarah, why do you continue to pull the worst kind of bad juju around you?" he said.

I continued to shiver and violently shake on the ground even with Teddy's added weight on my shoulders to prevent me from moving too much.

Mary huffed. "We gotta get this off. Hold her still."

She placed a hand on my lower back above the object and Teddy deepened his grip. Both inhaled before I felt the burning rip of metal tearing free of my flesh. I screamed. The metal prongs of the item clung tight and tried to dig deeper into my body. Mary grunted and pulled harder. A loud pop sounded followed by a clatter of metal on the wall close by. Wetness oozed over my exposed skin and dripped onto the cement floor.

Mary leapt up and sought out the thing and smashed it into pieces with her boots. Satisfied she searched the room for something to staunch the flow of blood on my back.

Cold continued to radiate throughout my body but it was no longer the sub arctic feeling. My muscles relaxed. On the edges of my subconscious I thought I heard an echo of something trying to talk to me. I shook my head and slowly sat up while I held my hand up against my forehead.

Just before I said anything the door to the supply room busted open and guards rushed into the room. We raised our hands in the air as the guards pointed their guns at us.

One said into a walkie-talkie, "We found them."

BACK DOWN IN THE CHAMBERS, the room was less crowded than before. The lines of humans waiting to be turned were gone along with the several creatures that oversaw the turning. Near the center under a light stood Vincent with Avarice next to him.

Around her neck was the small lamp and on her hip was a holster for the camera. My heart sped up when I locked eyes on the artifact. I needed to feel the smooth case in my hands again for my fingers itched for its warm embrace.

The two turned as the guards shoved us up the pathway with their guns. One snarled, "Quit dragging yer feet. I want to get out of here before their friends show up."

Avarice clucked her tongue at the guard. "Now, now. Let's give them a little dignity before they are turned into the living dead. It's the least we could do."

Our hands and feet were bound in rough rope that were

biting into our skin. Avarice opened her arms and walked up to me.

"Ah, Sarah, these artifacts are wonderful. Using the camera on yourself? Nullifying your tattoo? Transferring the djinn to this camera? Would never have thought of you capable of any of those things. Maybe you did have some smarts in that little noggin of yours after all. You've done well. Too bad you didn't modify your agreement with me or you wouldn't be in this mess tonight. You would have made a great partner. Oh, well." She sighed then patted my cheek.

I spat at her. Avarice swiped the spit away with her hand and wiped them on my top.

Mary interrupted, "'Scuse me. You did what Blondie?"

Avarice replied, "You heard me. Sarah moved the djinn from this lamp over to the camera. Though I'm not sure if he'll survive considering the nature of this camera. But oh well. This little turncoat djinn has been a pain in my back side for far too long. Now I don't have to worry about him since the camera will finish him off."

"How do you even know he's in the camera?" Mary asked and shifted her weight. "How do you know that the camera is not tricking you?"

A throaty laugh escaped Avarice's mouth. She smirked. "Because I have centuries of experience. You don't live as long as I have without being able to pick up on certain energies." She tapped the camera by her side and added, "I know for certain he's in this camera and I've been looking for this little traitor for quite some time ever since he helped stop the last apocalypse."

Wait, my old boss was older than her late sixties? I blinked and tried to adjust my eyes in the dim cavern but could not see past the older woman facade. While I pondered Avarice's actual age, I missed the conversation between her and Mary. I was brought back to the present when I saw Mary lean forward and motion at the camera.

"You're a fool." Mary narrowed her eyes at Avarice. "That camera will be the end of you."

Avarice primped the bun in her hair and said, "We'll see."

Vincent like the snake that he was slithered between us, at this moment, and rubbed his hands further south on me than I'd like him to and whispered in my ear. "Too bad you never made good on your debt with me sweetheart. It would have been fun."

"Fuck you." I spat at him.

He flicked it away and pulled me into a hard kiss. Once he let go he whispered, "Oh, if only."

Walter came around the massive column looking alive and healthy. His eyes hooded when he cleared his throat and asked, "Is this going to be long? I thought we had to clear out of here soon."

Walter? I thought he and his mother got the heck out of dodge. Was he working for Avarice this whole time? Were Mary and Seth, right? Things began to click into place and the roller-coaster swirled within my belly. Crap.

Avarice turned and smiled. "Oh that's right. We should get going before they get here."

"Who?" I asked.

"Someone had the audacity to call the meddlesome group of vigilantes called Wings of Virtue to our base. So, naturally I'm moving our base of operations. But before we head out we need to handle the loose ends. Which is you and your friends my dear."

Teddy interrupted, "Why not shoot us lady? It'll be far faster than doing the zombification."

"What? And not leave entertainment for our uninvited guests? I think not," Avarice replied.

She stepped away, walked towards the columns and clapped her hands. "Boys, if you would do the honors of strapping our guests in, that would be delightful."

Walter grabbed a hold of my ropes and yanked me forward. Vincent shoved Teddy ahead and pulled on Mary's rope. The guards stood back and held their guns at the ready. Their eyes scanned the room for any signs of trouble.

WALTER PULLED me over to the other side of the column and pushed me up against the granite surface. He bent down and undid the rope and lashed each leg into a strap then tightened them so I could not wiggle out of them. Next he shackled each wrist into the terrible restraints.

His gentle touch brushed against my skin, but he was different now. The once softness that he held in his gaze was gone. Instead, his eyes held a cold soulless quality to them. Walters's lips were pressed firm into a thin line while he went about making sure the straps were tight and allowed for no escape.

This was not how it was supposed to end. Me shivering and being shackled to the zombie column of doom by my husband. The one person who was supposed to have my back no matter what circumstances we were up against. Tears streamed down my face when I sobbed his name. "Walter."

He glanced up. A scowl plastered on his face. "What?"

"You look good."

"Yes, that's what happens when you are alive and have living flesh instead of being dead," he snapped back and tugged on the leather straps to make them tighter.

"Don't let her do this," I begged. "Please. You can stop her."

"No," he said. "Mother was right. You've been nothing but a toxic influence in my life. It's about time that I get rid of you for good."

"You don't mean that—"

"I do."

"But don't you love me?"

"Not anymore."

"Walter," I cried as my heart crushed inward and I sobbed. How could he be so heartless?

"Mother told me how many times you've sold me, and she's had to swoop in and pay off whatever ridiculous debt you've racked up for her to prevent me from being zombified."

"I only sold you twice," I argued.

"No. You've done it more than twice. Does thirteen ring a bell?"

I winced. Did I really sell him thirteen times? And how the heck did Glenda get wind of her son being sold to Avarice as my bargaining chip for overdue debt?

Walter leaned into me and whispered, "Sarah, Sarah, Sarah. Still the self-centered bitch that I know and once loved. You're not getting out of this... not if I have any say."

"This isn't you. Snap out of it Walter," I cried. Walter's hand whipped out and slapped me across the face. His steely cold gaze deepened his scowl.

"Shut up," he sneered. "For once I'm awake and can see past your conniving influence."

"No, Walter." I struggled against the restraints and tried to kick him. "It's your mother controlling you now. Wake—"

The resounding sting that followed the loud slap across my face silenced me. A coppery tang of blood covered my taste buds because I bit my own tongue. I spat the excess out on the ground and threw Walter a scathing glare.

Walter grabbed hold of my jaw and cheeks and squeezed hard while he said, "Don't you ever talk about my mother like that again."

Once he let go I replied, "You won't have to once this process is over."

"Good." He stepped back and turned. "My poor choice of a wife is now strapped down and ready for the transformation."

Avarice, who stood off to one side near a podium answered, "Excellent. Vincent, are you quite done with that annoying Wings of Virtue pest?"

"Argh," he replied. "She bit me. Hold still you little wench. Too bad I didn't have more time to break you."

"Vincent?" Avarice asked while arching an eyebrow. "Do hurry. We do not have all night."

"Yeah, yeah," he replied, grunting and yanking on the leather strap.

Mary yelped. "Watch it, asshole."

"You won't care in a few minutes sweetheart." He winked and walked over to where Avarice stood.

Teddy kept quiet on the other side and did not put up a struggle as the guards strapped him into place on the column. Once done, the guards and Walter all went to where Avarice stood and waited. From the shadows came a lone figure shrouded in a crimson cloak and held one of the long dark staves with an enormous bleached canine skull and within its maw held a ruby gem at the end.

The shadowy figure removed their hood and I recognized the dark hair that flowed down to her shoulders. Glenda covered the distance quickly before she took her place in front of the podium. Avarice and crew were stationed behind her and outside of the circle.

"Glenda?" I said, eyebrows creasing upwards. "What are you doing here?"

"To finish the job. With the goons that could cast the ritual gone because they ran off due to the oncoming threat, only I can cast the spell and my spell work is far more superior than their lengthy casting. What takes them an hour will be done in fifteen minutes." She sneered.

"You cast? Seriously?" I asked with more snark than needed. Glenda from what I remember was a terrible spellcaster. Maybe she had been practicing? Either way she was probably right she could cast the spell in less time that the minions took.

"Yes, you nitwit." Glenda growled. "Now shut up and accept your fate. I doubt your transformation will take long since you do not have much of a brain any ways."

Glenda glanced back towards Avarice, "And you promise to complete our bargain after I turn these three?"

"Yes." Avarice nodded. "Upon their zombification, I will

bestow upon you and your son the ability to become full blooded werewolves. No more will they shun you because you were half-breeds."

"Good." Glenda smiled and turned back to us. She stared me directly in the eyes. They were bright yellow. Full moon must have been at its peak tonight. Her sharp teeth were on display when she said, "I've been waiting a long time and now I shall enact my revenge on you dearie and get my rightful heritage after tonight."

Again, my mind reeled at the thought that Walter was a half breed too? He never exhibited any of the signs of being a were-wolf. What the absolute fuck, was all I could think of at the moment.

"You may begin." Avarice nodded her head and motioned for the she-wolf to proceed.

Glenda twirled the staff like a baton and worked her way around the circle. She growled, mumbled and hissed words that were not meant for human tongues. Eerie green lights emanated up from the sigils carved into the flooring and flowed upwards into the columns.

Her movements were different from the goblins' dance from earlier. Over to my left I heard Mary mutter, "Ivan you better hurry your sorry ass up or I will haunt you until the day you die."

I couldn't help but chuckle and shake my head. My worst nightmare was about to come to life and all I could do was laugh. The laughter became too much it bubbled up through my lips and echoed within the cavern while the laughter shook my shoulders and belly. Only the restraints kept me from falling on the floor as the hysteria overtook me into sheer madness.

Faintly to my right I heard Teddy say, "Hoo boy, she's finally cracked."

"She's been cracked for quite some time," Mary quipped. "That one wasn't running on a full load for quite a while now."

Mist rose from the holes in the ground and mixed with the light from the sigils. The wispy forms crawled across the floor towards our feet near the base of the columns. Glenda's chants became faster and she whirled the staff quicker as the ruby gem flashed red with each pound of the stick on the ground.

The mist wreathed in time like it had a pulse and snaked itself around our ankles and wrapped itself around our legs. Hissing sounded as the acrid cloud touched the fabric of our clothing. My laughter abruptly turned to loud screams when a searing sensation sank deep into my skin.

All three of us shouted, yelled and screamed until our voices became hoarse while the eerie fog swallowed us whole. I couldn't breathe without fire consuming my insides. Glenda was almost to the crescendo of the spell when a bright white flash exploded in the enormous chamber.

CHAPTER
THIRTY-NINE

A LOUD BEEP sound like that of an unhook life-support hummed in the background while I whacked at my ears to unclog them to stop ringing. I blinked my eyes from the sheer brightness of the room and looked around. I was no longer latched to the columns in the dark zombification chambers.

Instead, I stood in a white room with a person who looked just like me sitting on a stool. She wore all black and held her chin in her hand while her elbow was propped upon a knee. One eyebrow arched upwards while she took a long look at my battered form.

"You look like shit," she said.

"Zombification does that." I shrugged. "Kind of don't have control over appearance when you're being zombified."

She snarked back. "You're not a zombie yet, idiot."

"Pardon?"

"I'll say it slower." She scowled. "You. Are. Not. A. Zombie. Yet. Idiot."

"But I'm in the process of becoming one… unless…"

She shook her head. "No, dumb-dumb. You haven't been magically transported away to save your sorry ass from zombification."

"Then what the hell is this?" I gestured around the white room. "Where am I?"

"Your subconscious, genius."

"Why?"

"Because I have a message for you and I can only give these messages when you fall unconscious. The zombification ritual has done just that…"

"What good is a message, if I become a zombie?"

"Just stop talking and listen, genius."

She paused, shifted on the stool and examined her pristine nails. My real self never had pristine nails. In fact this subconscious me was way better looking than I was in real life. Trim and appeared to have her act together. My subconscious self looked up and said, "Are you done, yet? I don't have much time, because of what I know, you can stop yourself from becoming a zombie."

A surge rushed through me and I almost crumpled to the ground. The white room began to blink in and out of existence and I called out to myself, "How?"

"You must call upon Seth. Only he can help—"

The white room swirled as everything rushed back in on me and I felt sick. Pain bloomed in parts of my body and stole my breath away like a massive swarm of fire ants had engulfed my entire being and were tearing away at my flesh. The sound of skin burning and sizzling like bacon brought me back to the chambers. Only seconds had passed during the time I met with my subconscious. Glenda twirled then slammed the staff down on the floor in a resounding boom and the green lights in the floor flared to a brilliant light.

Trusting in my subconscious self, I choked and coughed out in desperation, "Seth."

———

The fog receded back down into the ground like ants going back into their hill until dinner time called upon them once again. Avarice stood at her podium with the low raspy laughter that erupted from her throat as she took the camera from her hip holster. She held the artifact in the air and waved it around.

"Whatever are you calling that turncoat for? He can't help you."

Her lips pulled wide and split into a malicious grin.

"I would say the zombification spell was working faster than usual but then again, you never were too bright, Sarah."

She brought the camera back down to her chest and caressed it before she continued, "I say this because you cannot control the djinn within this device. Only the welder of this artifact can control him. Which is me."

Warm wool-like cotton sensation began to wrap itself around the edges of my thoughts while the spell continued to work its way deeper. Perhaps seeking out my soul to bind myself to this undead nightmare. I fought against the temptation to just let go and have the warmth envelope my cold body.

A thought occurred to me. I rasped, "Aren't you afraid of the curse?"

"The seven day thing?" Avarice cooed. "Why not at all. I wasn't stupid like you and took my picture with the device. It has to capture your essence before it will bind itself to you and steal your lifeforce."

"Are you sure?" I asked. "From what I heard is that the camera doesn't care. It'll take your life regardless."

She waved a hand and dismissed me. "I know how to offset the curse and unlike you I'll do what's necessary... besides, I needed another form of punishment for the unfortunate."

A wicked laughter burbled out of her mouth once more and sent chills through me. Avarice's laughter died down when Glenda moved in front of her, presented the staff and knelt down before her.

"I've cast the spell of zombification as promised. The effects of the spell should be completed at any moment. These zombies will be more powerful than the others, compliant and far more deadly. Now it is time for you to hold up your end of the bargain" Glenda said.

The warm fuzzy feeling continued to encroach on my clear thoughts and I fought hard on the urge to give up. Avarice's eyes lowered, her hands still clasped around the camera.

Glenda added, "I've done all that you've asked and you've promised me this in exchange for my service on this night. I feel the full moon call to me..."

Avarice's long nails drummed on the podium before she

caressed the camera and said, "Djinn come out at once, for I command thee."

Gold hazy mist emanated out from the lens of the camera and sparkled to the floor catching the green and orange lights within the room. The mist condensed on the floor before it built upwards forming the seven-year-old boy that I knew from Mrs. Smith's house. Avarice arched her brow while the corner on one side of her mouth quirked upwards. She murmured, "Interesting."

Seth bowed before her and said, "Master, how may I serve you?"

"Djinn, dismiss this facade and show your true form," Avarice barked at Seth. He scowled before his body wavered and became hazy. The mist regathered into a taller form and materialized into the adult version with the well toned body.

He bowed once more and asked in a lusciously deep voice that would wake any dead libido, "Is this form more to your liking, master?"

The other corner of Avarice's mouth turned up as the coy smile spread upon her lips. She soaked in his form as she gazed up and down at him. Then said while she licked her lips in a slow sensual motion, "Yes, this will do."

"I aim to please, master." Seth bowed again.

"Avarice, remember? We have a deadline and we're running out of time. I'd like to become a full-blooded werewolf and leave with my son before those pests get here," Glenda said.

The silver haired woman turned to Walter and asked him, "Walter, before we continue, do you want to become full-blooded like your mother?"

He shook his head. "No. I prefer not to turn furry when the moon is full. Being a quarter-blooded werewolf is enough for me. I do not crave the power that my mother craves."

"Walter," Glenda shouted, shoving the staff onto the podium and stamping over to her son. She jumped then grabbed his ear and twisted it. "You will accept what is rightfully yours tonight and like it."

Walter twisted and ducked to get away from his mother. He held up his hands and said, "No, mother. It was never my dream to be a full-blooded werewolf. That was yours. I'm happy to be alive once again and not a maggot infested meat bag like my ex-wife will be soon."

"But Walter," Glenda whined. "A pack is stronger with family."

"No," he said and stepped back. "This is your wish. Not mine. I have other plans."

"Fine," Glenda huffed then squared her shoulders and walked back to Avarice. She said, "Forget my son. It will only be me that will accept the full-blooded werewolf heritage tonight."

"Fair enough," Avarice smirked. "Djinn, grant this half-blooded she-wolf her wish. Make her into a full-blooded were-wolf. In fact grant her the legacy blood."

Seth nodded. "As you wish."

Glenda clapped her hands, jumped up and down like a teenage schoolgirl while she squealed her delight at getting her lifelong wish granted. Though if she had owned the lamp before why didn't she ask for this wish? Was she too proud at that time to request it?

Seth directed Glenda to step away from the group and the

soon-to-be zombies. My ex-mother-in-law went to the far column and waited for Seth to work his magic. He held his strong forearms out in front of him, one over the other. His eyes glowed the fiery yellow while Glenda stayed put on the floor on all fours. Her entire being vibrated with eagerness.

No words were spoken. Seth merely blinked his eyes and nodded his head before magic transpired within the room. A thick magical wave that vibrated into the air and rumbled the ground and walls within the cavern. This magic rose the hairs on the back of my neck, had an off tang to it like it had turned sour or was twisted in nature.

Glenda gasped before her form crumpled to the ground as soon as the magic wave slammed into her. An outstretched hand twitched then moved before her nails shifted into claws. The rest of her flesh ripped away with fur sprouting all over her. Bones and tendons snapped and crunched while her body reconfigured itself into that of a wolf. Whimpers of pain faded into snarls of rage as Glenda's small form grew into a hulking form twice the size of a normal werewolf.

She held herself inwards before she threw her massive head back and howled which turned into maniacal cackling. "Mwaha-hahaha, yes, yes, yes. Finally."

She held her massive muscular limbs out in front and above her while she examined the razor-sharp claws that adorned her strong hands. Another elated howl escaped her lips, pleased with her new form. Glenda looked around the room and landed on Walter who stood next to Avarice. She lifted her lips to reveal the massive sharp wolf teeth and snarled at Avarice.

"Get away from my boy. He's *mine.*"

Avarice snatched the staff off the podium and spoke a series of syllables too fast for normal humans to even utter and some did not even have sound accompanying them. With a fast stamp of the staff on the flooring the green circle around the column came to life. The eerie fog weaved itself out of the ground faster than normal and wrapped around Glenda's legs and feet.

"What's this?" Glenda's eyes went wide. She tried to kick the diabolical fog away but it continued to cling to her fur no matter how hard she tried to shake it off.

She snarled and snapped at the mist but it continued to snake itself up over her. The fog covered her completely followed by loud howls of anguish. "Nooooo," Glenda bellowed and struggled to get away from the mist.

Avarice said, "Djinn, speed up the spell and make her mine."

Seth's jaw dropped. He stood there with his arms out in front, but he hesitated on completing the motion to make the wish become true.

Walter pulled on Avarice's arm and tried to take the camera. "But that's my mother."

"Do it now, djinn." Avarice growled and shoved Walter away.

Seth nodded and blinked to complete the transformation.

"No," Walter bellowed.

Glenda's werewolf form decayed before our very eyes as it became part of Avarice's undead army. An eerie howl erupted from the half-eaten maw of the werewolf before she glared back at us all with her glowing yellow eyes that had no pupils. The green lights in the circle died out, Glenda stood there and waited for Avarice's command.

"That's better," Avarice purred and patted Walter's cheek.

"You're better off without your dear old mother getting in the way all the time. Besides, I needed something to entertain our uninvited guests."

Avarice surveyed the room until her eyes landed on us. "Oh right, we have these three to finish... pity your mother was a terrible spell caster." She sighed. "No matter..."

With the dark staff in her hand Avarice turned towards Mary, Teddy and myself who were still in the process of being transformed into zombie minions. She raised the staff at us and said, "Finish them, djinn."

LOUD RUMBLING SOUNDED as the chamber shook and stalactite crashed down to the floor. Stone upon stone grated and crunched upon each other before light pierced the once dark cavern. A large hole was punched through one of the walls and in the opening was the silhouette of a dragon with massive wings.

Oh crap. Mrs. Smith. I could only hope the dragon didn't care for expired humans.

Seth stood there with his jaw hung open and dropped his arms when the dragon let out an ear-splitting roar. She spat fire into the room before she took flight. Behind her came the battle cries of several warriors that followed in her wake. They crawled over the opening and flooded onto the chamber floors.

Holy crap. When Mary called the calvary, she called the dang calvary.

Avarice shouted at Seth, "Turn them you fool. Do it now."

Walter lashed out and grabbed the camera from Avarice's hands and yelled, "No. I command that you do not turn them."

Seth furrowed his brow and stayed still. With two masters of conflicting commands he could not carry out either order. Avarice dropped the staff and shoved Walter, but he held onto the camera. The two continued to pull and yank each other's hair and wrestle over the camera.

Meanwhile the calvary continued to make their way to where we were held captive and slowly being turned into the undead slaves for Avarice. Thankfully Seth did not have the opportunity to make good on her wish when Walter stole the camera away from her.

In the front of the calvary was Ivan who called out to his troops to keep moving forward. Mary cried out, "Ivan! We're over here."

Ivan paused and stared at us before he pointed at Avarice, "Stop her."

People swarmed around him as the dragon dove down and took playful bites that missed over the two tumbling on the ground fighting for the camera. Vincent, recently unaccounted for, waltzed up to the rolling duo and snatched the camera from the ground.

Avarice and Walter gasped, "Give that back."

"I'm holding it for you, boss." He tucked the camera, using the lens, into the back part of his pants and ducked down as Mrs. Smith did another pass overhead.

Avarice shoved Walter aside and spoke unsaid words before she slapped his forehead. Walter fell limp on the floor as his head rolled to one side. She stood back up and dusted herself off, unperturbed by the encroaching army of people.

Ivan and crew were halfway across the room before Avarice snatched the black staff off the floor and whirled it around. The butt of the staff smashed into the ground and a green light flashed outward in the chambers with a loud boom.

Avarice cackled. "Arise my darlings. Now is the time for you to prove your loyalty to me."

More and more my eyesight began to cloud over as the spell took a hold of me more and fought to consume my living spirit. The stubbornness deep within did not give way not even an inch. I clenched my teeth and screamed to fight the spell.

Underneath our feet the floor rumbled to life. The ground began to crumble as the earth shifted while hands broke free of the once rock solid chamber floor. Hundreds upon hundreds of the undead rose up from the ground. The calvary that consisted of only one hundred people was against all odds now.

Avarice's voice boomed through the room while she held the stick above her head and pointed at the calvary. The zombies and werewolf waited her orders. "Now kill."

Immediately chaos ensued. Screams and cries of pain or terror erupted from the living. The undead chanted in long drawn out moans for brains. Except the werewolf. Her eyes turned berserker red and she dove into the fray and whipped around like a blender. Blood spattered everywhere along with body parts and bits from unfortunate souls that got in her way. She also tore into the zombies that were stupid enough to stay within her warpath.

The zombies that were only partially risen grabbed ahold of

unsuspecting victims, who were rushing to where Mary, Teddy and I were held captive, and pulled them down underground. Their screams echoed throughout the expansive room.

Over to my left I heard Ivan's voice. "Mary? Mary?"

The sound of skin being slapped resounded before he asked again. "Mary? Come back to me. You're stronger than this. Fight it off."

Mary said in between labored breaths, "Can't. Too strong. Need Seth."

"Seth?" Ivan asked. "Seth who?"

"Djinn," she replied. "In camera."

"Not a lamp?"

"No. Camera," she wheezed. "Hurry."

Bright fire lit the room as Mrs. Smith torched several of the zombies like dried kindling. Their bodies burned while they continued the assault on the other Wings of Virtue members. The numbers of the living were quickly dwindling. I felt my heart begin to slow upon realizing that we might not win.

Ivan fought with a machete that he brought with him and hacked through the opposition. Avarice and Vincent were gathering up Walter when they noticed that Ivan was almost upon them. My old boss took two of her fingers to her mouth and blew a shrill whistle.

Glenda paused mid-strike. Her ears moved to face us. Avarice pointed at Ivan. "Get him."

The zombie werewolf leapt into the air, flew over the zombie horde and landed in front of Ivan blocking his way. He sucked air in between his teeth and spat, "I do not have an issue with you girl. Move aside and I will fix you."

Oops. Bad choice of words. Glenda's ears flattened to her scalp, her fur bristled and a deep guttural growl bubbled through her canine lips. She lowered herself, ready to pounce at the slightest movement that Ivan might make to get around her.

Avarice wove her hands and Walter's body levitated in the air in front of her. She turned and said, "Vincent, stay. Make sure these degenerates do not follow."

Vincent nodded, "Of course."

Walter's floating form disappeared into one of the dark tunnels with Avarice guiding him with the dark staff in the other hand. Vincent watched while he kept an eye on Ivan who was currently occupied with an angry werewolf. Meanwhile, the zombification spell took a turn for the worse. I felt it fraying the edges of my consciousness as it threatened to make my brain into Swiss cheese.

Mary called out in a raspy hoarse voice, "Ivan, camera. Demon has it."

Vincent held the camera in his hand. His fingers caressed the case as he cocked his head to one side. His lips mouthed the words, "I wonder."

Ivan, not oblivious, dove to one side, nearly missing the razor sharp claws, to go after Vincent before he had a chance to call up the djinn. Glenda rose up and howled. As she thrusted her body up into the air and arced after Ivan, I saw the fiery breath of the dragon before the talons pieced the zombie werewolf in mid-jump.

The werewolf let out a shriek as Mrs. Smith reached around and opened her ginormous dragon maw and bit down on the werewolf's head with a sickening crunch. I felt nauseous. Guess the dragon did like expired jerky after all. Blarg.

At this point my vision faded to a bleary gray. Sounds, smells and vibrations enhanced all around me. I fought hard to stay away. Not too far away I heard the sound of plastic and metal clatter to the ground. The men shouted and struggled as they pounded each other's flesh.

Mary called out, "Ivan—"

Her voice cut off in an eerie silence until the next moment the grave chilling moan escaped her lips. Deep inside I felt the darkness grow and ravish the rest that lived. Breathing became labored as my heart shuddered to a complete stop.

FORTY-ONE

I FELT weightless as I hung outside my body and watched Ivan cry out for Mary. He slugged Vincent once more, knocking him out. Ivan rolled Vincent's body off of him and lifted himself off the ground. He walked a few feet, searching the ground, and found the camera. Still in one piece.

Ivan scanned the room. The undead were dwindling into piles of flaming ash. About a quarter of the calvary survived and were making quick work of the remaining zombies with the help of the fire dragon, Mrs. Smith.

Before me I took one look at my body and shuddered. The spell had done the work and converted my once healthy flesh into months of decay. Flesh hung from dried tendons and holes were bored into the body exposing dried up organs and worn bones.

I no longer had a nose and the nasal cavity was on display for all to see. My once perfect lips were non-existent as a permanent snarl exposed my teeth. Fingers moved and curled into claws and tried to slash at any Wings of Virtue member who wandered too close to my undead form.

Ivan called over to the idiots. "Back away. They are undead and will bite into your flesh with no remorse."

The one member that was close to me backed away and tripped over a stone that fell earlier during the whole battle. Other members were behind Ivan and binding Vincent's hands and ankles to make sure that he wouldn't escape anytime soon. The dragon landed and transformed into the elderly woman facade.

She approached Ivan with her hands out. "Give that to me."

Ivan pulled it away. "No. This camera does not belong to you."

"You promised" she argued. "My help for any artifacts found on the premise."

He shook his head. "Not this one. Sarah owns it."

Mrs. Smith put her hands on her hips and huffed. She eyed my zombified form and replied, "She's dead. Give me the camera."

"I will give you something else," he replied. "Anything else."

"Fine." She held her breath for a moment then exhaled. "Your truck."

"Betsy?" Ivan's brows rose upwards. He replied, "No."

"Yes."

Ivan glanced between her and us. His hand clenched tighter on the case. Seth, materialized before them, his eyes narrowed to slits and said, "Do it."

A slight groan emanated from the grown man before he agreed.

"I can undo the spell," Seth offered and gestured at me. "All you need to do is wish."

Ivan bit his bottom lip and shifted the camera in his grip. "How do I know you will not twist the wish? I've heard bad things about djinn. You are not to be trusted."

He looked over at Mrs. Smith who glared back at Seth. Seth shrugged, "It is in my nature to shift the powers or to add a spin on the wish but in this instance I have the same wish as you. Save these three."

Finally Ivan nodded, "Do it. I wish for you to undo the zombification spell and bring them back to life."

Seth turned towards us and got close. He held his forearms up in front, then nodded his head while he blinked. "As you wish."

Another wave of power emanated from Seth and shot towards our rotten bodies that were kept in place by the leather straps. I held close to Seth in my ghost form and watched the magic worm itself into our dead flesh.

Gold and white sparkled while the magical light swirled around the damaged flesh and mended the open wounds and mummified parts. The gray pallor that accompanied our undead complexion was slowly replaced by healthy pinks. Mary's form gasped for air as her eyes blinked awake.

She turned towards Ivan and said, "Oh, hell, here I thought I was dead."

Ivan chuckled and undid the leather straps on Mary's hands and feet. "No. You're a strong girl, Mary."

Mary quirked an eyebrow. "Girl?"

He raised his hands up in defense. "Woman. I meant a strong woman."

Teddy sputtered next. "My god, I need some new clothes. Does anyone have some pants I can have? I don't like standing here in my voided bowel, thanks."

Mary and Ivan both laughed as Ivan motioned for one of the members in the Wings of Virtue to help Teddy out of his restraints and gain some new clothes.

Meanwhile, Mrs. Smith walked up to my unconscious form, leaned forward with her nose close to my chest, inhaled deeply and said, "This one is still dead."

Seth was watching Ivan, Mary and Teddy but whipped his head around. "What?"

The elderly woman gestured to my limp as a noodle form with healthy flesh hanging from the straps with no indication of waking up from my dead sleep. Seth marched over to my body and shook me.

He said with each shake, "Wake up."

A slight vibration radiated through my ghostly form. Tiny strands clung to me and led me back to my physical form. Ivan moved Seth aside and undid the straps before he laid me down on the floor. He began CPR. First several compressions on my chest before he breathed air through my mouth.

The strands pulled me closer but some began to snap. I was unsure if I wanted to stay. This was my chance to leave all of this behind. But did I want to?

CHAPTER
FORTY-TWO

"NOT SURE IF you want to leave?" a voice said to my right. I jumped. The woman was clad in all black and wore feathers in her bright red hair woven into tight intricate braids. Piercing blue eyes complimented her stark white skin. The bridge of her nose sported a smattering of cute freckles. She was about my height.

She twisted her braid and said, "Sorry. I did not mean to startle you."

"Are… are you death?" I asked warily.

The woman laughed. "No. But you could say in part that I am. I'm a Valkyrie."

"Valkyrie?" My eyebrow shifted in denial. "You handle the warriors that fall in battle and escort them to Odin's table for a forever feast."

"Yes," she replied and kept watch on my physical body. "In the past, yes. But no more. Valkyries of today are tasked with helping the dead."

"Oh."

"Do not fear. I am not here to make you leave. For it's your choice." She turned to me then glanced up and down.

"Wait, I have a choice?"

"Yes. This time around, you do."

"Why?"

"I cannot tell you."

"Then what if I choose to stay dead?"

She frowned. "The world will burn."

"Wow. Seriously?"

The Valkyrie nodded.

"Talk about doom and gloom. And here I thought I was a total nobody."

"You were…" She worried her bottom lip. "Before you picked up the camera."

"That cursed thing?"

"Yes."

I was speechless. One cursed camera took me from some unknown nobody who wanted to escape the supernatural world to the only one that could stop the earth from burning. The one thing that I wanted more than anything was to be rid of my debt to the supernatural mafia and to be normal. Death offered just that peace.

But, I felt the tug of responsibility pull me the other way. Deep down I couldn't let the world burn. Cursed camera or not, I needed to get back and stop whatever force wanted to destroy life on earth.

The Valkyrie looked into my eyes with her piercing blue one and asked, "So, have you decided?"

I bobbed my head and walked over to my physical form that laid on the ground. Ivan continued to pound on my chest and breath air into my lungs. Seth hung in the background and watched with uncertainty.

Before I reached out the Valkyrie grabbed my wrist. I stopped and glanced up. She pointed over at Seth and said, "That one. Watch out. He means well but like you he will do what he has to in order to survive. Even if he likes you, he will betray you... unless...."

"Unless?" I asked.

"You bind him," she replied. "Even though the camera has Solomon's ring, it does not control that djinn. Why? I do not know."

"How do I bind him?"

She smiled. "You make a wish."

SETH PUSHED Ivan out of the way and took over CPR of my lifeless form. I saw tears form in his eyes as he continued to do each compression and breathed air through my lips.

He said through clenched teeth, "Come on, come on. Live dammit."

With each pound I felt the strands pull me closer and yank hard to bring me back into my physical body. The Valkyrie stepped back and nodded her head before a whirlwind of feathers swirled into existence and a raven flew away.

I laid my ghostly form back into my physical body and felt Seth continue to pound on my chest. Ivan's low voice rumbled, "She's gone djinn. Let her go."

"No," he cried and clung to my lifeless body. Ivan tried to pull him away, but he shrugged him off to pound away on my chest. His lips pressed down on mine as he blew air into my lungs. I felt the warmth flow through my cold body and swirl with tingles.

Seth said in a low whisper, "I will not let you die. Not after I've found you after all these years. You will not die on me."

He drew back and continued the compressions and came back to breathe more life into my lungs. I returned the light brush with a kiss of my own. His kiss lingered longer on my lips and deepened. Magic coursed through my veins while he worked to bring me back to full life.

Pain bloomed on my right arm as the tattoo tried to break free of the camera's restraint. Seth worked his hand down my arm and a cooling sensation followed in its wake. The burning cooled then dissipated when he lifted his hand away and held my jaw.

I reached up around his back and used him to help me back up into a sitting position. Breathing in through my nose to continue our sensual kiss before he broke away. He caressed the side of my cheek and said, "Hey. Thought I lost you."

"What?" My eyes searched his.

Seth narrowed his eyes and huffed. "You truly are not that bright, are you?"

"Stop with the blonde jokes and kiss me again."

His eyes danced with delight and leaned back toward me. "As you wish."

The power of our kiss emboldened the magic deep within me as I remembered the Valkyrie telling me that he needed to be bound or else face betrayal. Having enough betrayal, I wished, mentally, for Seth to be bound to me and the camera.

Magic coiled outward like a golden snare. The tendril

wrapped itself around the djinn around his chest and pierced through his heart. His fiery eyes widened when he realized too late that the magic at work entwined and bound him to me. Seth broke away from the kiss and exclaimed, "What did you do?"

"I did what needed to be done." I replied. "Bound you to me."

"No," he said and dropped me. "Impossible."

His lips thinned to a hard line. "You have no powers to bind me."

"I had a little help." I wiggled my fingers and pointed at the camera. He snapped his head back towards Ivan who still had the camera in hand.

Ivan shook his head and replied, "I did no such thing djinn."

"Then how?" Seth's brows creased upwards.

I smirked. "Consider it my death wish."

His brows creased together, realization blooming across his face, and quickly narrowing his eyes. "You saw her? The woman that turns into a raven?"

"The Valkyrie? Yes."

"What did she tell you?" he glowered.

I worked my mouth into a thin line. Not liking the string of interrogation coming from my djinn. "Let me say this, I'm tired of betrayal."

The look he shot me, with his liquid gold eyes, doused me with a heavy dose of cold. I shivered on the ground. He moved backwards onto his haunches still pinning me in my spot with a lethal glare.

"I would never have betrayed you," he said, the corners of his mouth turning downwards into a fierce frown. "By bounding me to you, my powers have been diminished. Which is not good, because you're a magnet for trouble and you need my protection. On that note, I'll have to be one to make sure you keep a clear head then I have no choice."

He snapped his fingers and his adult form changed back to that of a seven-year-old boy with short blond hair and amber eyes. My jaw dropped. All that hunky glory, gone, in a flash.

I got up and hustled over to Ivan and snagged my camera from his grasp. I said in a firm voice, "Seth you will return to your adult form right now, if not immediately."

"No." He stuck his tongue out at me and dissipated into the golden mist that sparkled in the light. The mist wafted in the air and moved towards the camera and entered in through the lens.

I shook the camera and yelled, "Get out this instant, you little brat."

He spoke in my mind. *Fat chance of that happening. You may have bound me, but you have not taken my will. Though, you won't have to worry about betrayal anymore but mark my words I will be as difficult as possible from this point on. I won't forgive you for binding me Sarah. Not for a long long long time.*

I let out a long sigh then looked around. The remaining cavalry for Wings of Virtue were spread out in the chambers administering healing to the wounded and doing last rites for those that had fallen. Teddy came up to me and asked, "So, you and the djinn, huh?"

I flushed. I sputtered, "No."

"Are you sure?" he asked. "You and he were playing hockey

with each other's tonsils for quite some time. Made me think there was something going on between the two of you."

Heat crept up to my ears. They must have been beet red.

Seth chimed in, *"You and I? That's ridiculous. Girls have cooties. Bleh."*

I shook the camera and mumbled, "Shut up."

Teddy quirked an eyebrow up. "Problems?"

"No. None at all." I bent around Teddy to get Ivan's attention. "So, what now?"

Ivan rubbed the back of his neck and surveyed the room. "We finish up here and then head back to headquarters."

"Not in my truck you don't," Mrs. Smith sneered.

He threw his hands up in the air and rolled his eyes. "Of course, I was not going to take your truck Mrs. Smith. I will call an Uber if need be."

"Good." She toddled over to a member who needed her help and assisted in tending to a severely wounded person on the ground.

Teddy asked before I had the chance. "Say, does your group have some sort of facility that Sarah and I can go to? Or at least a couch or sofa that we can crash on?"

Ivan massaged the back of his neck and was about to answer when I saw Mary.

"No, Ivan, no." Mary bustled over to us. "A hundred times, hell, no."

"But Mary, it is our way. Help those who need help," he said.

She sliced the air in front with her hand. "No."

"Like it or not, it is our way." Ivan argued then nodded. "Yes.

We might have a few places that you can stay until you get back on your feet."

Mary continued to shake her head and wave her hands while uttering several no's. Ivan's smile grew wide to show his white pristine teeth. "You can crash at Mary's place."

"Oh, hell, no," Mary whined and hung her head. Ivan laughed.

EPILOGUE

It had been weeks since I took residence on Mary's couch. She wasn't the best of hosts, but I wasn't the best of guests either. Teddy had gone with Ivan when we left the chamber and Ivan helped him get his motel back up and running. The things that the Wings of Virtue did was amazing.

Mrs. Smith indeed got to keep Ivan's truck Betsy until he was able to offer a far better prize in exchange for his beloved scrap of metal on wheels. Don't get me wrong. I loved driving Betsy around for those few days, but the girl had a temper. If you didn't change gears just right, then she would up and stall out on you no matter how fast you were going.

As for me and Seth? Let's just say that the djinn was still throwing his temperamental fit over being bound to me and the camera. He said his powers were diminished due to being bound and he felt betrayed because I had the guts to do such a thing to him. Seth continued to show up in the seven-year-old form and I was getting used to it.

I brushed my hand over the camera to ask one question that continued to bother me. First, I had to check to see if he was willing to talk. I asked, "Seth, are you still not talking to me?"

"No." He sighed. *"What do you want?"*

Remembering that night sent chills through me but I pushed forward and asked, "Why didn't Glenda make her wish to be a full blooded werewolf when she owned the lamp?"

"She didn't trust me and I don't blame her. A djinn could twist any wish from their master. To the point the wish could result in their untimely deaths. Whereas you, you're an idiot and make wishes without fear of the consequences."

My stomach dropped upon realizing that a single wish could kill me. But then again, I did change the dynamics, and Seth was bound to me, so if I died, then so did he, right?

"But if I died, wouldn't you as well?" I asked.

"You right. That's why I haven't twisted any of the wishes. My own self-preservation is what is keeping your dumb-ass alive."

Thinking back to Glenda and her gory fate, I continued with my bevy of questions, "So, why did Glenda allow Avarice to make the wish for her?"

"She didn't know that Avarice was going to make the wish. Glenda assumed Avarice had another artifact to change her, like she had many artifacts to change people into zombies of various tiers."

"Oh." I said, leaving my mouth in an o shaped form.

"Sarah, what the hell are you doing?" Mary whacked me over the head with a couch cushion. I tried to bat it away.

"Chilling and sating my curiosity. Why?" I asked.

"Weren't you supposed to be going to an interview right now?"

"Was I?"

"Yeah." She grimaced. "You were. I thought you would have left by now."

I shook my head and held up my hand. "It's not an on-site interview. It's virtual."

Mary did a double take when she noticed that I still wore pajama bottoms but the upper half of me wore work casual clothing. I snatched Mary's laptop off the coffee table and opened it.

She objected. "Hey. That's mine."

"You want me to get a job, right?"

"Not with my stuff."

"Can it," I replied. "Or you can expect to have me sleeping on your couch for another week or two."

She growled and threw her hands at me while she walked away. "Whatever, blondie, whatever. Keep the stupid laptop if you get the job. Whatever gets you out of here faster."

I snickered and opened my email then found the interview zoom address. I clicked on the URL which opened up the virtual meeting. The interviewer was waiting and immediately greeted me when I logged on.

The interview went on for two hours and I met with several team members that were eager to quiz me on various skills needed for this job. Though some were distracted and kept on hearing coworkers exclaim for them to go look out the window. At the end the recruiter told me that they'll be in touch soon with the yay or nay. I thanked her but my curiosity got the better of me and I asked, "What are they looking at?"

The interviewer responded, "There's some crazy stunt some movie or show producer are doing, the town square is flooded with zombies."

"Zombies?" I replied, a chill trailed down my spine. "That's crazy."

"Yeah, totally." The interviewer agreed. "Well, it's been nice, but I got another meeting to go to and all. Bye."

The interviewer ended the call. I blinked, exited out of the virtual meeting, reached over and closed the laptop.

With a deep breath I exhaled. I really needed this job. An SEM (search engine marketeer) associate position did not offer much but it was a start. A start to a completely normal and boring life. Where I could go into an office, zone out and look forward to office outings that revolved around how much beer and alcohol I could drink.

Pretty much life after college type of life which is what I craved. Avarice hadn't come sniffing around or sent any of her undead minions after me. I suspected she wanted to steer clear of the Wings of Virtue. At least I no longer had the enchanted tattoo on my arm. Seth completely obliterated it when he woke me up from my death slumber.

Mary came back into the room and tossed keys at me and said, "Done? Good. You're driving this time."

"Where are we going?" I asked and glanced at the keys she had thrown my way. Oh goodie, the slug bug. Another vehicle even more persnickety than Betsy. I groaned, placed the camera and laptop back on the table then got up. "Er, let me go change and grab Seth."

Mary shook her head. "Nope. Don't have time."

"Ah come on. I don't want to mess up these clothes. The last time I couldn't even wash out the goo that soaked into the fabric. I had to throw that clothing out. Besides, Seth's binge watching the *Real Housewives* so it'll be a moment before we can hustle on out."

"Tough." She waved at the door. "Grab your shoes, the streaming junkie and let's get going. We've got a situation that needs your camera's special skills."

"Where?"

"An old warehouse. Supposedly has a nest of ghouls hiding out in it."

I groaned. Ghouls. If there was anything worse than zombies, it was ghouls. Almost as fast as vampires but way more gross and gag inducing because of their rancid bodies.

"Seth," I called down the hallway. "We gotta go."

"But it's just now getting good." He whined.

Mary added, "Tick, tock, blondie."

Ignoring Mary, I rushed over to the far side of the room where I had a stack of plastic totes that held clothes donated by several members of the Wings of Virtue. I snagged some jeans, a t-shirt and steel-toed boots then changed into them.

"SETH." I yelled. "Get your butt over here."

"Ugh, do we have to?"

I copied him and asked Mary, "Do we have to?"

Mary simply stood by the door and tapped her shoes and kept glancing at an imaginary watch. I snarked back at her, "Fine. But those ghouls aren't going anywhere and I'm not going to get their nasty sludge all over my nice clothes because you've got a bee in your bonnet. So, chill."

She was about to say something when her phone rang. Mary plucked it out of the holster and answered, "Ivan, what's wrong?"

Mary stood there with the door open and listened. Her brows furrowed as she sucked in air through her clenched teeth. She replied, "Oh, hell, no. You've got to be shitting me? Seriously?"

She nodded then ended the call and said, "Forget the ghouls, blondie. We've got to get downtown and help Ivan. Another zombie horde has broken out."

We both hurried out the door while I snatched my camera up from the table.

Seth called behind us, "For the love of… can't a demon watch a show in peace?"

His golden mist form followed and flowed into the camera. His presence scanning my mind and said, *"'Bout time. Avarice finally decided to show her face again?"*

"Seems like it, Seth," I replied as I ran and hopped into the slug bug then fired it up. The souped up engine roared to life and we squealed tires as we sped out of the driveway and down the road. Mary hung on for dear life as we turned the corner and then stopped abruptly.

In front we were met with a wall of the undead. Hundreds of them if not thousands. Mary and I both said in long drawn out vowels, "Oh, hell, no."

AUTHOR NOTES

MARCH 3, 2024

So, how was it? Did you enjoy the story? Are you looking forward to the next one? Can I hear a 'hell yeah'?? Cool, cool. My favorite character is Mary. Her no nonsense attitude and "Oh Hell No" has gotten me through many horrendous workdays. How about you? Which character is your fav?

I hope you'll be revving to read book two of the series. I've inserted the blurb at the bottom of these notes.

RECENTLY I'VE LOST TWO BELOVED FRIENDS...

Back in October 2023, I lost my sweet dear Bubba. Bubba was a happy go lucky Pomeranian, and NOTHING got him down. He was my social butterfly and enjoyed visiting with everyone. Bubba called everyone his friends and loved them with all his heart. His life was filled with happiness. Though tragedy struck, he was fifteen, cancer was rampant and the doctor agreed the quality of life wouldn't be the best. So, yes, it was a tearful and difficult decision to let him go in peace. I still miss him.

Most recently… on February 29, 2024, I lost Zeke. He was our rescue Green Cheek Conure, turquoise color - one of the rarer variations, and came to us from our mechanic. We were Zeke's only hope because his owner could no longer keep him. Let me tell you, Zeke, when he first came to us, his little heart was broken. But little by little we helped him mend with love and care. He was a bright and curious fellow who enjoyed watching the birds outside, loved to fly around the house and sit with me while I worked. Every morning when I'd greet him he would say my name. I still miss his greetings and him being my constant shadow. This month would have been his hatch-day month. He was going to be fifteen :(but alas, it was his time to venture over the rainbow bridge to join his friends who had already passed on before him.

I'd like to believe Bubba and Zeke are reunited with their family and friends up in heaven. They will be there to greet those who come after them and cherish the reunion. I look forward to seeing them again.

May both babies know they are loved and may their spirits run and fly free.

FINALLY, THANK YOU'S ARE IN ORDER...

Thank you Nola, Nadine, Karen, Dorcia and Bryan for needling me to finally publish this story. I probably would have sat on this for another two to three years.

Nola, thank you for your keen eyes in finding big semi-truck plot holes and your recommendations on how to fix them. Also, thanks for not letting me get distracted again.

Nadine, thank you for listening to my waffling decisions of what to write and when to publish.

Karen, thank you for the continued push AND for listening.

Dorcia, thank you for editing the story and ensuring the dreaded 's' I continue to add to 'regards" get removed. I have no idea where I picked up that habit, but thank you.

Bryan, thank you for reading the story.

I truly appreciate each and everyone of you!

Until next time, I hope you have happy days full of memories to cherish for years to come.

~A.L. Scarborough

SHADOW BOUND CHRONICLES

NIGHT SHIFT - BOOK 2

In the heart of the bustling city lies The Glen, a store within a mall where shadows hold secrets darker than night. In the second installment of the Shadow Bound Chronicles, Sarah is thrust back into the supernatural world, her hopes for normalcy shattered by mysterious murders gripping The Glen. Cast out from the Wings of Virtue society and entangled in inter-dimensional intrigue, Sarah and her enigmatic companion Seth confront malevolent forces as they unravel the sinister truth: the apocalypse is underway, and Sarah's cursed camera holds the key. As they bear witness to unimaginable horrors during their shifts at The Glen, they realize the fate of all worlds hangs in the balance. In a desperate race against time, Sarah must embrace her destiny and confront the threat lurking in the shadows. Will they uncover the truth before The Glen becomes a tomb for all who enter?

Be the first to grab your copy here:
https://www.aliciascarborough.com/al-scarborough/book/
Shadow%20Bound%20Chronicles/Night%20Shift

ALSO BY A. L. SCARBOROUGH

UNDER THE NAME OF ALICIA SCARBOROUGH

https://www.aliciascarborough.com/alicia-scarborough/series

Mystical Mishaps Series

Potion of the Hound (Book One)

Rise of the Vampire Brethren (Book Two)

Making the Mark (Short Story)

Becky the Pantry Ghost (Short Story)

The Volkrog Princess (Short Story)

Children of Chaos Series

Play with Me